DOWN FROM BEAST MOUNTAIN

GERRY GRIFFITHS

SEVERED PRESS
HOBART TASMANIA

DOWN FROM BEAST MOUNTAIN

ISBN: 978-1-925711-46-2

DEDICATION

For my loving wife, Marilyn

1

Billy Boggs heard it banging around inside the dumpster the moment he stepped out the rear door of the Porterville Steakhouse. He cursed himself for neglecting to close the cover and secure the lid with the padlock the last time he had dumped the trash earlier that afternoon.

Gordy, his tyrant of a boss, swore the next time another mangy animal climbed inside the damn dumpster because it wasn't locked up, and scattered garbage all over the back parking lot, he was going to plant his boot so far up Billy's ass he'd be tasting shoe leather, and hire a dishwasher that knew how to listen and follow instructions.

Billy was bone tired and his black shoulder-length hair was slick with sweat from the steamy kitchen. His apron was crusty with food stains, and his Converse sneakers reeked of cooking grease, a smell that permeated his nostrils even when he wasn't at work.

He dropped the two garbage bags he'd been carrying on the ground.

Whatever was inside the dumpster was too preoccupied rummaging for its next meal to notice Billy standing just fifteen feet away.

He glanced up at the single floodlight mounted just under the eave. Tiny moths were clinking against the yellow bulb, which cast an insipid glow stretching to the edge of the woods and over the only two vehicles remaining in the rear parking lot, which were Billy's beater Honda Civic and Gordy's Ford F-150 truck.

Billy knew if he didn't hurry up, Gordy would come storming out to see what was taking him so long as his bad-tempered boss was probably through adding up the receipts and would want to lock up and go home so he could kick back in his Barcalounger with a bottle of Jack Daniels.

Billy considered his options as the animal continued to dig through piles of trash.

He could sneak up, toss in the garbage bags, and slam the lid down.

This time, he'd make sure the dumpster was locked.

But if he did, he was afraid that the animal would suffocate. He remembered Gordy telling him the day they delivered the dumpster that his boss had purchased this particular brand because the manufacturer claimed it had a hermetic seal and would contain any foul odors.

Which Billy knew to be a bald-faced lie as the putrid container smelled worse than a crapper pit in a Porta Potty, especially in the summer months.

Even if the animal could breathe, Billy was pretty sure the ammonia and other toxic smells would be overpowering enough to kill it. Something he knew all too well as Gordy was always yelling at him not to mix chemicals whenever he scrubbed down the urinals and toilets in the restrooms. Billy knew Gordy could care less if he dropped dead from the fumes. Gordy was more worried about the bad publicity and if folks would even want to eat in a place where an employee had died in the restroom.

Leaving the scavenger in there to die seemed cruel, but it was sure better than getting fired.

Or maybe it would be simpler to just go over and politely shoo it away. But that didn't always go as originally planned as he'd learned from experience.

Once he'd tried to scare off a raccoon that was skulking around the back of the restaurant, but the animal hadn't been so easily intimidated. Instead of hightailing, the belligerent raccoon had attacked him; almost tore off his hand.

When it finally let go, the raccoon scampered off around the side of the restaurant in the dark and got run over by a car as it tried to cross the road.

Luckily for Billy, Sheriff McGuire had shown up when he did and bagged up the dead raccoon. He rushed it over to the Medical Center, and after the lab tech performed a quick brain autopsy, it was determined that the animal's aggressive behavior was most likely due to an ornery mean streak, and not rabies, saving Billy from the ordeal of having all those shots.

It took twelve stitches to sew up the nasty wound and left a cool scar on the back of his hand that he liked to think looked more like a tattoo.

He glanced down and noticed that a seam had split open on one of the bags when he had dropped them on the ground and some gross mush had leaked out. He knew if he attempted to lift the bag, the bottom would fall out and there would be a big mess, which would be a disaster, especially if Gordy were to come out and see garbage spilt everywhere.

Using the toe of his sneaker, he shoved the food scraps back inside the bag. It smelt awful but he had developed a strong stomach spending all those long hours working in the back of the kitchen dealing with other peoples' unwanted food and scraping off their plates.

Billy bent down and slipped his hand under the bag to support the bottom. He stood and walked gingerly toward the dumpster, holding the bag in front of him, ready to heave it over the rim of the refuge bin. He raised the bag higher…

The rear door banged opened and a gruff voice yelled out, "Boggs! Get the hell in here and finish up!"

A menacing growl bellowed from the dumpster.

Then the contents of the garbage bag exploded in Billy's face.

He didn't even have time to close his eyes.

Blinded and covered in goop, Billy stumbled and fell on his back.

"Thanks a lot, you son of a bitch," he swore, wiping gobs of mashed potatoes from his eyes as he looked up.

A large shape vaulted out of the dumpster, landed on two feet, and dashed into the woods.

2

Kit Tanner closed out the register and looked up at the clock. It was almost nine o'clock. It had been a long day at her grandfather's store. Wiley Tanner had just turned 72, which wasn't old by any standards, but his arthritis had pretty much crippled his hands so he couldn't run the Porterville Hardware and Hunting Supply all by himself like he used to, which was why her mother, Bess, worked there five days a week and Kit helped out whenever she could.

"Thanks again for lending a hand," Wiley said as he came out of the backroom and joined Kit behind the counter.

"Is Mom ready yet?" Kit asked.

"Got plans?"

"No. Not really. Just tired."

"Well, you did put in a full day," Wiley said and patted his granddaughter lightly on the back with his gnarled hand.

"Have you seen my keys?" Bess Tanner said, coming over from the gun section of the store.

"They're right here where you left them, next to your purse," Kit said, pointing to the ring of keys on the glass counter.

"Right you are," Bess said. She looked at her father-in-law. "You all right to drive?"

"My hands might be a couple of crabs but they can still steer me home."

"Night, Grandpa," Kit said, heading for the rear exit door.

"Get plenty of rest," Wiley said. "Expecting a big shipment tomorrow."

"See you in the morning, Dad." Bess gave Wiley a goodnight kiss on the cheek.

"See yah."

Kit held the door for her mother and they went out to the back alley where their car was parked. Bess opened the driver's door on their Volvo station wagon and unlocked Kit's side.

Main Street was quiet as they drove by the Porterville Supermarket and a few of the smaller storefronts, which were all closed for the night.

A light was on at the sheriff's office.

Kit stared out her window and saw most of the homes along the way were dark and everyone had already turned in for the night. Such was the daily life in Porterville; a backwoods town nestled in a narrow valley of pine forest at the base of an imposing mountain range.

The Volvo bumped over the railroad tracks and passed by the Porterville Steakhouse. Kit tried to be discrete and snuck a glance, hoping to get a glimpse of Billy outside getting into his car.

"I see you looking over there," Bess said.

Kit faced forward and stared out the windshield.

"I don't know what you see in that boy."

"Billy's not what you think," Kit said.

"No?"

"He's a good person."

"That why he associates with the Levitt brothers?" Bess said.

Kit noticed her mother speed up as they reached a straightaway.

"Billy's nothing like them." Kit glanced over at the speedometer and saw the needle steadily arching up the gauge to 50 miles per hour. "Mom, shouldn't you slow down?"

Bess turned and looked at Kit.

Kit clutched the harness strap on her seatbelt with her right hand and placed her left hand on the dashboard as they thundered down the road. "Why do you hate him so much?" She looked up and saw that her mother was still staring at her.

"I don't hate the boy…"

"Mom, the road!" Kit yelled.

"…I just think you can do better."

A hunched figure lumbered out in front of the car.

"Mom! Look out!"

The front bumper scooped the body onto the hood and sent it careening into the windshield, spider-webbing the safety glass, as it tumbled over the roof.

Her mother slammed on the brakes and the car skidded off the road.

Kit screamed as the Volvo slammed into a tree.

3

Sheriff Abel McGuire stood on the shoulder of the road and watched the ambulance speed off with its siren blaring and the flashing emergency lights illuminating the surrounding trees like a carnival midway.

He strolled by his Ford Crown Victoria cruiser and left his light bar flashing just in case other cars might happen by.

Bud Tinker from the local Texaco gas station and wrecking yard was rigging a chain to the frame just under the Volvo's back bumper.

"How's it coming along? Need some help?" Abel asked. Bud was getting up there in years having run the town gas station for the past half-century. Abel would feel a little strange if he didn't ask if he could lend a hand even though he knew the stubborn old man would just decline the offer.

"Just about there," Bud replied, rattling around the undercarriage. He finally stood and straightened his back.

Abel could actually hear it crack.

Bud took his time and climbed up the embankment. "Mrs. Tanner sure looked in a bad way."

"Yeah, she was still unconscious when they put her in the ambulance," Abel said.

"What about the daughter?"

"Kit? She was pretty shaken up. I'm sure she'll be fine."

"Any idea what caused them to crash?" Bud asked.

"Kit said they hit an animal then went off the road."

Abel leaned against the side of his cruiser and watched as Bud went over to the control box on the side of his truck and started up the winch. The motor hummed as the cable drew taut and the car was dragged slowly back onto the road. The cable continued pulling the car until it was on the tilted flatbed of the tow truck. Once the vehicle was all the way on, Bud pulled a handle and the flatbed leveled out.

Abel walked over and joined Bud at the back of the tow truck. Abel flicked on his flashlight to examine the damage to the front of the car.

"I'd say she's pretty much totaled," Bud said, clacking his dentures.

Abel had to agree. The front grill and bumper were U-shape from wrapping around the tree. The hood had buckled. The shattered windshield was bowed in and looked like someone had painstakingly glued thousands of tiny shards of glass together. There was a crease on the roof where the animal had bounced off the top of the car.

"Is that blood?" Bud said, pointing up at the bumper.

"Looks like it," Abel said. "I better get a sample." He walked back to his cruiser and popped the trunk. He generally kept the cargo compartment fairly organized. Besides the spare tire and jack, it was where he kept his two twelve-gauge Remington pump shotguns for backup and a duffle bag filled with a few boxes of cartridges and other law enforcement supplies. He leaned in, opened a small forensic kit, and grabbed a clear evidence bag with a Q-tip applicator inside.

He came back, swabbed the still-damp blood with the Q-tip, and slipped it inside the baggy.

"So what're you going to do with that?" Bud asked. "Send it off to one of those fancy labs."

"So it can get lost in the shuffle? Nah, I'll have Lucy look at it."

"If you ask me, it was a deer. Damn things cause more wrecks."

"You're probably right."

"How's that dog of yours?"

"Cooper? He's just fine." Abel turned and let out a short whistle.

A black Alsatian sat up in the back seat of the cruiser. The dog gazed out the window for a brief moment then lay back down.

"He's not much of a police dog, is he?"

"Coop's more of a sidekick; keeps me company."

"Well, I best get this wreck to the yard," Bud said, getting in his truck. He stuck his head out the window. "See you later, Sheriff," he hollered and drove off.

"Later," Abel replied. He hooked his flashlight on his utility belt and started walking to his cruiser.

He was about to open his door when he heard something skulking in the bushes behind him and then it stopped. He grabbed the grip of his service revolver but didn't pull the gun out of the holster.

He slowly turned around and set his thumb on the hammer.

It was too distracting with emergency lights strobing, so he reached inside the car and turned them off.

Everything went pitch black.

It took a few seconds for his eyes to adjust.

He removed his flashlight from his belt but didn't turn it on. He was sure if he waited long enough, whatever it was that was out there would soon make a break for it.

A twig snapped.

He clicked on his flashlight and shined the beam in the direction of the sound.

A dark shape rattled the leaves as it darted behind a long string of bushes then bolted deep into the forest.

Abel heard a low guttural growl behind him.

He slowly glanced over his shoulder.

Cooper was sitting up in the back seat, ears perked and fangs bared.

"Well, that got your attention."

4

Grant Tanner pulled up onto the gravel driveway and noticed right away that Bess' Volvo wasn't in its usual spot. He parked his work truck next to the garage, turned off the engine, and switched off the headlights. Grabbing his lunchbox off the bench seat, he climbed out of the truck, and walked over to the front porch.

He'd decided to work late at his office in town and catch up on some paperwork that he had been neglecting. His duties as Porterville's Fish and Game warden had been keeping him rather busy working out in the field, issuing fines and making sure fishermen and hunters were obeying the regulations.

He unlocked the front door and went inside.

The house was dark.

He turned on a lamp and ambled across the living room to the kitchen. He felt along the wall, found the switch, and turned on the overhead dome light in the middle of the ceiling.

He looked up at the clock on the wall. It was after eleven o'clock. Bess and Kit should have been home long ago.

He never liked for them to be out so late, and often warned them about the potential dangers, insisting the Volvo be gassed up so they wouldn't have to stop on the way home at night to fill up.

He reached inside his trouser pocket and took out his cell phone. After scrolling down his contacts, he dialed the hardware store. He let it ring until it went to voicemail and ended the call.

"Where is everyone?"

He was about to call his dad at home when the house phone on the wall rang.

Grant picked up the receiver. "Hello?"

"Grant, this is Abel."

"Abel, what are you—?"

"There's been an accident. Bess and Kit were taken to the Medical Center."

"I'm on my way," Grant said and slammed the receiver on the cradle.

He ran out of the house, not bothering to lock up and dashed out to his truck. He fired up the engine and tore down the driveway in reverse, kicking gravel everywhere.

Grant shaved the normal twenty-minute drive down to ten minutes and skidded to a stop by the curb at the main entrance to the Porterville Medical Center. He hopped out and ran around the front of the truck. He dashed toward the automatic sliding glass doors and managed to slip through before they had even opened all the way.

He raced through the small lobby by the unoccupied information desk and up the flight of stairs two steps at a time to the second floor.

There was no one at the nursing station. He could hear voices further down the hall coming from one of the rooms.

He rushed over and stood in the doorway.

Bess was lying on a hospital bed, a thin white blanket covering her chest. Her left arm was out protected inside a plastic splint. A bandage covered her forehead and was wrapped around her head. An IV tube stuck out of her other hand and ran up to a drip bag hanging on a stand. A machine *blipped* as it monitored her heart rate and blood pressure.

Dr. Kate Wilson was noting something on a clip chart while Nurse Vera Rivers adjusted the bed to make sure Bess was lying flat.

"Where's Kit?" Grant asked.

Dr. Wilson looked up and gave him a reassuring smile. "Oh, hi, Grant. She's in the waiting room."

"Is she hurt?"

"Just some scrapes and bumps. Thank God they were wearing their seatbelts."

"What about Bess?"

"She took a blow to the head and broke her left arm just below the elbow. I'm going to put it in a proper cast in a bit."

Grant gazed at his wife's face. Her eyes were closed and there was a clear oxygen mask over her nose and mouth.

"But she's okay, right?"

"Well, she was unconscious when the paramedics brought her in. She hasn't woken up yet."

"So what happens now?" Grant asked, feeling like he needed to lean on the doorjamb. It was time to talk to his father and insist that he shorten the store hours.

"We wait. You should go check on Kit. She was pretty upset when they were brought in. I've given her a sedative to help calm her."

Grant stepped away from the doorway. He turned and went down the hall to the waiting room. The door was open.

Kit was sitting on a faux leather couch, staring up at the blank screen on the television mounted up near the ceiling in the corner of the small room furnished with another identical couch, a coffee table with some magazines, and a snack vending machine.

Grant stepped in and sat beside his daughter. "Thank God you're all right."

Kit turned and faced him. Her eyes were red and her cheeks were streaked with mascara from crying. "It was all my fault."

"What do you mean?"

"We were arguing and she wasn't..." Kit leaned in and Grant put his arm around his daughter as she started to sob.

"It's okay. Everything is going to be okay," Grant assured her.

Nurse Rivers appeared at the doorway. "Mr. Tanner?"

"Yes," Grant replied.

"Your wife is awake."

Grant smiled at Kit and gave her a big squeeze. "See, what did I tell you?"

They got up, rushed down the hall, and stepped into Bess' room.

Grant went around one side of the bed while Kit stood on the other side to be next to her mother, whose eyes were closed.

He looked over at the doctor who was standing near the door. They'd known each other for years, even went to the same high school.

"She's nodding in and out."

"Grant, is that you?" Bess said in a low voice.

"Yes, dear," Grant said, leaning down over his wife. "Kit and I are right here."

Bess opened her eyes and gazed up at Grant. "Tell her I'm sorry..." and then her eyes closed.

"Bess?" Grant said but when she didn't respond, he shouted her name.

"Grant, I doubt if she can hear you," Dr. Turner said. "We should let her rest."

5

"How long will she be out?" Grant asked, standing with Kit by the nursing station as they discussed Bess' condition with the doctor.

"I'm hoping not long," Dr. Turner replied. "Bess has a concussion. There's a small chance she may have a cerebral edema."

"What's that?" Kit asked.

"It's cranial pressure to the brain."

"Is it serious?"

"Well, we won't know until we've run some tests. If it is a cerebral edema, it's just a matter of time waiting for the swelling to go down."

"And what if the swelling doesn't go down?" Grant asked.

"The only option would be to operate," Dr. Turner said. "But like I said, we're hoping it's just a concussion. There's nothing you can do at the moment so why don't you two go home and get some rest. We'll call you if there's any change."

Kit looked at her father. "Grandpa was counting on us being there tomorrow."

"Well, I don't see any reason you can't go."

"But what about Mom? I want to be here when she wakes up."

"Don't worry, I can pick you up in the afternoon and bring you here so you can sit with her." Grant glanced up at the clock. "Will you look at the time? I better get you home."

"Like I said," Dr. Wilson said, "we'll call you if there's any change."

"Thanks," Grant said. He put his arm around Kit's shoulder. They walked down the corridor toward the stairs.

A minute later, Abel appeared around the corner with Cooper at his side. The German shepherd spotted the doctor and galloped down the hallway toward the nursing station.

"You know, we do have strict rules against dogs in the hospital," the doctor said.

"Are you referring to my deputy?" Abel replied with a smirk.

Cooper went up and sat at the doctor's feet. He raised his right leg and pawed the front of her white lab coat.

"Hold on." The doctor grabbed a pet dish off a shelf from under the counter. She went over to the water cooler and filled up the bowl then put it on the floor. The dog lowered his head, lapped up the water, and didn't stop until it was all gone.

"You should be careful, he was dehydrated."

"I know. Got stuck out on the road longer than I expected. Saw Grant and Kit as we were coming in. Grant told me Bess has a concussion," Abel said.

"That's right."

"Is she going to be okay?"

"I think so."

"Well, that's a relief." Abel stepped around Cooper and stood in front of the doctor. He bent down and kissed her on the mouth. She responded by cupping the back of his neck and pulling him in closer.

Once their lips parted, Abel said, "So, Kate, did you miss me today?"

"Well, I don't know. Haven't seen you since breakfast and you did call me three times." She gazed into his eyes and grinned. "Yeah, maybe a smidgen."

"A smidgen, eh. Not a tad?"

"I don't know, which one is smaller?"

Abel shrugged, the motion making the edge of the plastic evidence bag poke out from his uniform shirt pocket.

"What's that?" Kate asked.

Abel took out the bag. "It's a blood sample I got from Bess' car bumper. Thought maybe Lucy could analyze it for me."

"Sure, I'll make sure she gets it," Kate said and took the evidence bag.

"Well, I think Coop and I are going to call it a night."

"I'll be there soon."

"Come on, boy," Abel said, and started walking down the corridor.

Cooper hesitated and stared up at Kate.

"You heard the sheriff."

The Alsatian spun around and bolted down the hall after Abel.

6

"I've spoken to Dr. Madison about Bess. He's in his office if you need him. See you later," Kate said, slipping on her coat and heading down the hall to the rear stairwell.

"Aren't you going the wrong way?" Vera asked, standing at the counter of the nursing station.

"I promised Abel I'd give this to Lucy," she responded, holding up the evidence bag.

"Night," Vera said.

Kate passed the service elevator used for transporting patients on gurneys and delivering medical supplies. She pushed open the fire door and took the stairs down to the ground floor. She opened the door and stepped into the hall. The bottom floor was dimly lit, as the laboratory and the x-ray departments were both closed.

She went over to the drop box mounted on the door to the laboratory and slipped the evidence bag inside along with a short note for Lucy Banks, who was both the lab and x-ray technician for the hospital. Even though Lucy was often swamped, she always made time for Kate, especially if it had to do with Abel's work as she had always shown an interest in forensics and was a big fan of all the CSI spin-offs.

Kate turned and looked down the hall at the service door that led outside to the rear dock used primarily by personnel in the coroner's office and the funeral home.

Normally, the exit sign over the door would be lit up with red letters but tonight it was blank. She walked down the corridor to take a look.

She stopped at the door marked MORGUE and jiggled the handle. She was relieved to find it locked, and had a key, but had no real reason to go inside.

She approached the service door. A thin outline of light shone through from the outside. She grabbed the push bar and pulled it toward her. The door clicked shut.

Somehow, the door had been left ajar which was strange as it was also an emergency exit with an alarm. So why hadn't the alarm triggered? Could it be an electrical problem? She wondered if anyone had reported it.

Kate made a mental note to notify the maintenance department on her next shift and was about to leave when she spotted a small control box next to the door. She reached up and opened the front lid. Inside was a panel with a single switch. It was in the off position. Kate flipped it up and the letters on the exit sign over the door lit up.

"Well, that was an easy fix," she said with a smile. Someone had deactivated the alarm and forgotten to turn it back on.

Satisfied that she had resolved the problem, Kate turned and walked the other way down the corridor and left the building.

7

Billy got up early the next morning in hopes of catching Kit before she went into work. He rummaged through his dresser drawers until he found a clean enough T-shirt and a pair of jeans that didn't have permanent food stains all over them. He came out of his room and went down the short hall. His parent's bedroom was on his right. He opened the door and looked at the made bed, the room just the way they had left it, the day they were tragically killed when a big-rig truck plowed into them head-on.

Fortunately, there had been a life insurance policy that automatically paid off the house so he wouldn't have to worry about making mortgage payments; and as he had just turned eighteen, he was allowed to live on his own and not be forced into child protective custody.

But there were still unpaid bills that needed attention, some of which he was able to pay off before the balance of his parents' savings account went to zero.

Billy was struggling working menial jobs.

Halsey Levitt and his brothers had learned of Billy's dilemma and loaned Billy two hundred dollars, and like a fool, he had taken it. When he tried paying the money back in small installments, Halsey told him not to worry about it, that there were other ways he could pay off the debt.

And now he was in their hip pocket.

Billy slipped out the front door and climbed into his Honda.

Even though he'd never buy one for himself and thought it was extravagant, Billy decided to surprise Kit with a specially brewed espresso.

He headed over to the supermarket and drove into the parking lot to the Coffee Mill, a coffee kiosk drive-thru near the entrance by the street. He could smell the tantalizing aromas as he pulled up. Lottie Brand greeted him with a big smile from the window.

"Well, hi there, Billy. Don't see you much."

"I'll take a caramel mint mocha."

"Coming right up." Lottie began preparing the drink.

Billy remembered Lottie from when he was going to school. She'd been a grade ahead of him at the time.

She was wearing a nametag: LOTTIE and her title BARISTA beneath.

He almost had to laugh. She was a year older and had been an honor student in high school and here she was serving people coffee. Didn't seem that much of a step up the ladder from bussing tables and washing people's dishes.

"There you go," Lottie said and handed a paper cup with a lid out through the window.

Billy hadn't expected the cup to be so hot and almost dropped it. He immediately fit the cup in the holder on his console.

"That'll be four dollars."

Billy pulled the ashtray out where he kept much of his change. He counted out the correct amount and handed the coins to Lottie.

"Thanks, Billy. Have a nice day."

Billy nodded and drove off. He went past the supermarket, made a turn, and went into to the back alley behind the Tanner's store. He parked fifty feet away from the rear door and shut off his engine to wait.

Wasn't long before Grant Tanner showed up in his official work truck and let Kit out. Billy waited until the truck was gone before he got out of his car. "Hey, Kit, wait up!"

Kit was at the door and turned around. "Billy, what are you doing here?"

"Brought you something." Billy held out the paper cup.

"This isn't a good time."

"What do you mean?" Billy asked, swapping the cup into his other hand as it was scolding hot.

"My mom's in the hospital."

"Why, what happened?"

"We got into a car accident last night."

"Jeez, I'm really sorry…"

"It was all because of you."

"Me?" Billy could tell Kit was upset and wasn't going to accept the cup of coffee so he put it down on the ground as it was burning the shit out of his hand. He stepped toward her.

"I really don't want to talk about it right now." Kit turned, put her key in the lock, and opened the door.

"Kit, wait."

Refusing to listen, she slipped inside, and shut the door in his face.

"I got your favorite," Billy said.

He was about to walk over and retrieve the coffee cup on the ground when a four-door off-road truck with high-suspension, camouflage paint, heavy-duty bumper brush guard, and oversized all-terrain tires barreled down the alley right for him. He jumped back as the truck came to a stop. The left front tire rolled up on top of the paper cup and squished it flat. Brown liquid spewed out all over Billy's sneakers.

He looked down at his soaked Converses then glared up at Halsey Levitt grinning back at him from the open driver's window as the rumbling engine vibrated the body of the truck.

Halsey was an imposing man with a tanned, weathered face and a full beard. As always, he was geared up for hunting, this morning wearing a red flannel shirt and a hunting vest.

"Dumb place to leave your coffee," Halsey said snidely. "Wouldn't you boys agree?"

Cobb Levitt leaned forward in the front passenger seat and looked at Billy but didn't comment. Even though he was the youngest and was often pushed around by his brothers, Cobb didn't let it make him a callous person. Billy felt sorry for him, but what could he do? Lately, he too, was getting the brunt of it.

"I doubt that little girlfriend of his is even old enough to drink coffee," Rand Levitt commented from the back seat. He had a blue bandana covering the top of his head and his goatee was so long that he'd tied it in a braid.

Rand was sitting next to their family pit bull named Grover, which was sixty pounds of pure muscle. Grover growled and snapped his teeth. White drool slathered everywhere as he struggled to jump out the window while Rand playfully restrained the dog, letting it advance then pulling it back.

Billy prayed the dog didn't pull out of its collar.

Three hunting rifles with high-powered scopes hung on the gun rack mounted over the rear window. A large animal transport cage was in the bed of the truck along with some folded tarps, and two large 75-quart ice chests with casters and pull handles.

Halsey stared at the rear door of the hardware and hunting supply store for a moment then looked directly at Billy.

"You know what I think you should do?" Halsey said.

Billy didn't like where this was going. "No."

"I'd like a key to that store."

"There's no way Mr. Tanner is going to give you a key."

"No, I don't suppose he would. But you could get your girlfriend's and make me a copy."

"No. I'm not going to do that."

"That's pretty tough talk. How about I let Grover take a bite out of you?"

"Just say the word," Rand said, smacking the pit bull on the rump to rile him up even more.

Billy took a step back. Even if he ran, he knew he'd never reach his car in time before Grover chased him down. He knew the dog was vicious. He'd witnessed Grover attacking a cat once. As soon as the pit bull had its first taste of blood, there was no stopping it from ripping the cat to shreds.

Halsey leaned out his window a little. "Billy, come over here."

Billy knew not to trust Halsey and hesitated.

"I said, come here."

Even though he knew better than to listen to Halsey, Billy took a couple steps toward the truck.

"Closer, Billy. Don't make me have to yell."

Billy took another step.

Halsey's hand shot out like a rattlesnake strike, grabbing Billy by the T-shirt and slamming him up against the truck door.

"I'm going to say this once, and only once. Get me that key!"

"And what if I can't?"

"Billy, quit with the shit. I know where you live."

Billy shook his head.

"You wouldn't want anything bad to happen to that nice little girlfriend of yours, would you?"

"You better not hurt her."

"Then get me that key." Halsey pushed Billy away, revved the powerful engine, and the big truck roared out of the alley.

Billy stood there for a moment before walking over to his car. He didn't know what felt worst: being bullied by Halsey Levitt or getting snubbed by Kit.

This certainly wasn't how he thought he'd be starting his day.

8

Billy drove around to the rear parking lot of the Porterville Steakhouse and shut off his engine. He got out of the Honda and went inside. Right off the bat, he could smell the distinct aroma of seared meat as Gordy warmed up the griddles. Not only was Gordy the owner, he was the cook.

"Billy, you're late," Gordy boomed, stepping out of the walk-in freezer, carrying bundles wrapped in white butcher paper.

"Sorry," Billy said, even though he was actually five minutes early. He kept on walking, pushed through the swinging doors, and entered the dining room.

Penny Styles was standing at the counter in her waitress uniform. She was filling up salt and pepper shakers on a tray.

"Morning, Penny." Billy went over and started taking the chairs down off the tables. Each night before he left, one of Billy's many jobs was to stack the chairs so he could run the vacuum around. In some spots, if the customers had spilt a beverage or ground food in with their shoes, he'd have to shampoo the insidious maroon carpet with its series of brown diamond shapes and gold royal crowns in the centers.

He sometimes wondered if people were as sloppy at home as they were when they came to the restaurant.

"Hi, Billy. Would you put these on the tables for me?" Penny screwed on the last metal top on a glass salt shaker.

"Sure." He didn't mind helping Penny because she was a hard worker just like himself and wasn't one to slough off her responsibilities onto him. Plus, she often stuck up for him whenever Gordy started to get on his case. His boss knew when to back down, as Penny was an ace waitress and was great with the customers, and certainly not so easy to replace, unlike a menial dishwasher.

The dining room was fair size with twelve tables that could seat four, six of them lined up against the windows facing out into the front parking lot.

Penny had her own system when taking orders and never got flustered no matter how hectic things got, especially when it was a bustling full house.

If a large party of people came in, Billy would put some tables together on quick notice in between bussing and wiping down tabletops for the next patrons. Penny was always gracious and split her tips with Billy as he worked equally hard to ensure every customer had that Porterville Steakhouse culinary experience.

Penny was standing in front of the chalkboard, which listed a limited menu; another reason the restaurant was able to offer prompt service. She erased the portion size and the price on the bottom selection, and substituted the new ones in her neat handwriting, so the menu looked like:

PORTERVILLE STEAKHOUSE
(Includes mashed potatoes, gravy, and assorted vegetables)
T-BONE 10 ounce $12.99
PORTERHOUSE 12 ounce $13.99
SIRLOIN TIP 10 ounce $11.99
RIBEYE with peppercorn sauce 10 ounce $14.99
GRILLED BONE STEAK 20 ounce $10.99

"What is a grilled bone steak?" Billy asked, looking at the last entree.

"I don't know. Gordy put it on the menu. Probably some old meat he's trying to pass off before he has to throw it out," Penny replied.

Billy carried the tray around the tables and set out the shakers while Penny followed behind and put out new napkins and clean cutlery. Penny stopped and held up a knife.

"What's wrong?" Billy asked, noticing that Penny was scrutinizing his work.

She twirled the knife in her hand, examining both sides.

"Did I miss something?" The last thing he wanted was for a customer to make a big stink saying there was dried food on their utensil and demanded to see the manager.

Penny closed one eye and frowned.

"Okay, give it to me." Billy put down the tray and held out his hand.

Penny looked at him and grinned. "Billy, I'm just messing with you. It's spotless." She laughed and continued arranging the place settings on the tables and moving the candle glass holders to the center of the tables. She would light the candles a few minutes prior to opening.

"Penny!" Gordy yelled from the kitchen.

"Yes?" Penny hollered back.

"Tell Billy to get in here and start making the potatoes."

Billy looked at Penny. "Why doesn't he just ask me himself?"

Penny shrugged and shouted back. "He'll be right there!"

Billy pushed through the swinging doors. He walked by the walk-in freezer, which was now padlocked, and passed the six-burner stovetop. Gordy already had a large 32-quart pot of gravy simmering under a low flame.

Various types of meat were marinating in glass trays on a countertop next to the griddle so Gordy could throw on a steak the second Penny specified the cut and placed the order slip on the turnstile next to the pass-thru into the kitchen.

Billy grabbed a heavy 60-quart pot off a shelf and put it on top of an unlit burner.

Gordy had already laid out an industrial size bag of frozen potatoes to thaw on the cutting block next to four large boxes of powdered mashed potato and a box of powdered milk for Billy to mix with a few cups of water and heat up.

As soon as Billy got the mashed potatoes going, he pulled down another 60-quart pot and half filled it by dumping in some frozen mixed vegetables from a bag and some water.

Billy always thought it seemed deceitful, tricking customers into thinking they were eating freshly prepared food, but no one seemed to complain.

Gordy said the trick was smothering everything with his very own special recipe home-style gravy and serving it up with a fat juicy steak.

Billy couldn't argue there.

The cook did have a way with meat.

He could magically transform a bland piece of liver and make it taste like a mouth-watering filet mignon.

Gordy Oxman was a definite wizard when it came to the kitchen.

9

Grant's truck left a swirling cloud of dust behind as he rambled along the dirt road and weaved through the dense forest. Twenty years ago, logging trucks would have been barreling down the same narrow road, transporting fresh-cut timber down to the Porterville sawmill. But after the mountainside was nearly stripped clean, it was decided that it was time to close down the operation. It took all that time for a secondary forest to take hold and mingle with the old-growth trees still left standing and hide the scars of all the logging trails carved on the face of the mountain.

He spotted a dusty Ford sedan parked off the shoulder and pulled in behind the vehicle. Grant grabbed his daypack, got out of his truck, and locked up.

It was chilly, so he wore his official parka with the Fish and Game patch on the right sleeve, along with his usual attire: brown ball cap, UV protective sunglasses, brown shirt, green trousers, holstered nine millimeter semi-automatic, and hiking boots, just so there was no mistaking he was a game warden.

He'd planned a full day in the field and packed a 16-ounce metal water bottle, a couple cheese sandwiches, an apple, his citation book, and a GPS tracker that he was required to carry at all times but never had any reason to use as he was familiar with the terrain having grown up near the mountain.

He climbed an embankment and strode up a dirt path that stretched up through the trees. Carrying the rucksack over one shoulder, he trekked up the gradual upward slope and glanced about, breathing in the clean crisp air, and listening to the sounds of the forest.

The trail veered to the left to avoid a cluster of boulders and traversed back around, continuing up the side of the mountain. Grant spent many hours hiking through the forest so he was in top physical shape.

As he walked, he studied the ground up ahead. From what he could tell from the boot prints, two people had passed this way before him.

He continued on for another twenty minutes until he reached a shelf of rock that bordered a small meadow. He could hear a babbling brook and knew Dibble Creek was just up ahead.

As he approached, he saw a man and a young boy with their backs to him on the bank of a cove by the fast-moving stream.

The man cast into the water and took the slack out of his line as he bottom fished.

Holding his pole with both hands, the boy sat on a rock and watched a red bobber drifting in the rippling water.

Grant knew never to sneak on people and called out, "Hi, there!"

The man immediately turned around with a startled look then his expression changed to concern. "Hello." He immediately started reeling in his line.

"Are we in trouble?" the boy asked, looking over his shoulder.

Grant gave the boy a friendly smile and strolled down. He waited until the man had reeled in his line and placed his pole in a holder staked in the ground. "Mind if I see your license?"

"Sure, I have it right here." The man unbuttoned his shirt pocket, reached in, and pulled out a laminated card. He handed it to Grant.

After looking it over, Grant said, "Everything looks fine here, but there is a problem. This is a catch and release area."

Grant glanced in the water and saw two rainbow trout on a stringer lying still in two feet of water, but still moving their gills. "I'm afraid you're going to have to let them go."

"I'm sorry, I didn't know," the man apologized.

Grant saw that the boy was beginning to get nervous. "No need to worry."

"But I don't have a license."

"How old are you, ten?"

"Eleven."

"You still have another year. For fresh water fishing, a person needs a license after they turn twelve." Grant looked over at the man. "Mind if I look at your gear?"

"No, go right ahead. Tommy, you better reel in your line."

Grant examined their tackle boxes. After he had completed looking through the trays filled with hooks, sinkers, and lures, he checked the baited hook on the end of the boy's line.

"If you want to fish here, you'll both have to use barbless hooks. I noticed that you have a packet in your tackle box. Normally, I would cite you but I'm going to let you off with a verbal warning."

"Thank you. Like I said before, I had no idea that this was catch and release."

"Let's get these guys back to what they were doing." Grant stooped and reached into the water. He undid the tie and passed the metal threading needle back through each of the fishes' gills, hoping they weren't too exhausted to swim away. But they were resilient. The thick-bodied trout kicked their tail fins and propelled back into the rushing stream like they were late for the party.

The man took a pair of nail clippers out of his tackle box and cut the hook from the boy's fishing line. He was in the process of attaching a barbless hook when he said, "You know, we heard gunshots not so long ago."

"Which direction was that?"

"Farther up the mountain. Don't like hunters so close while we're down here fishing."

"Well, they have no business being up there in the first place. Hunting season's not until another two weeks," Grant said. "I trust if you catch any more fish you'll set them free?"

"We will," the man promised.

"You and your boy have a good day."

***

Grant checked his watch. He'd been hiking for an hour and hadn't seen anyone out hunting. Instead of stopping to eat, he'd been snacking as he went along so he could cover as much ground as possible.

It was time to head back to the truck.

He was working his way down a steep slope and was about to reach a spot where it leveled off when he spotted something suspicious—a deer leg dangling at the end of a rope, hanging ten feet off the ground from an overhead tree branch. The hide above the hoof was swarming with flies.

Someone had formed a pile of leaves directly below the hanging bait.

Grant found a large rock and tossed it into the middle of the heap.

The leaves burst into the air as an enormous set of metal teeth snapped shut with a loud, powerful *clang*.

Grant grabbed a long stick and prodded the ground as he warily approached the tripped bear trap. It was old and rusted. A metal stake had been driven into the ground to anchor the heavy-duty chain attached to the stock end. The trigger device was rather nicked up, which meant that it had seen plenty of use.

Judging by its size, Grant figured the bear trap had to weigh 40 pounds.

Even though leg-hold, kill-type, and snare traps were illegal in the state, the penalty using one was like a slap on the hand as fines never amounted to more than a $1000 and jail time never exceeded 30 days, which only made Grant's job more difficult as the punishment never seemed harsh enough to dissuade anyone from committing such a heinous act on an animal.

Resting on one knee, Grant took a closer look at the closed jaws and saw pieces of brown fur and bits of dried meat stuck to some of the metal.

He swiped the bridge of the trap with his fingertip. He rubbed his forefinger and thumb together and studied the smudged residual blood.

Even though the blood was dry, it still looked rather fresh.

He doubted if it could have been more than two days since the animal was ensnared and the trap was reset.

The bear trap was too ruggedly built to destroy and he was damned if he was going to leave it there to be used again on an unsuspecting animal.

A C-clamp bolt ran through the hole in the stock end and connected the heavy chain to the stake driven into the ground. Grant unscrewed the nut on the end of the bolt and removed the chain.

He picked up the 40-pound bear trap, even though his truck was a good hour-long hike away, and lugged the contraption down the mountain.

10

Rand was on his belly staring down from the ridge, watching the game warden start down the mountain. Halsey scooted next to him to take a look.

"It'd be an easy shot from here," Rand said, placing the man down below in his gun sights.

"We kill Tanner and this mountain will be crawling with lawmen. Besides, he's never going to catch us."

"Been trying long enough." Rand ducked back. "Shit, he looked up this way."

Halsey lowered his head. They waited for a moment then Halsey peered down through the trees. "He didn't see us. He's gone."

They moved away from the edge and walked over to the monster truck parked just off the dirt road. Rand leaned his rifle against the rear tire and stepped around to the back of the truck. Halsey grabbed a can of beer out of the cab, popped the tab, and joined Rand.

A bedroll of butcher tools was laid out across the width of the tailgate so they could select the proper cutting instrument when needed. There were various carving and skinning knives with different length blades and sharp pointed fillet knives for slicing perfect cuts of meat, a kitchen axe, and two bone saws.

Cobb was a few feet away by a tree, one hand on the trunk as he leaned down and puked one more time. He finally stood straight and wiped his mouth with the back of his hand.

"What's up, little brother?" Rand said. "Not feeling so well?"

"Leave me alone," Cobb replied.

Rand rolled up his shirtsleeves just past his forearms. He grabbed a bloodstained butcher's apron that looked like it had been salvaged from a slaughterhouse, looped it over his head, and tied the back strings. He slipped on a pair of cut-resistant gloves and fastened a painter's mask over his nose and mouth.

After perusing the assortment of knives, he chose the best skinning knife. He walked over to the large animal lying in the dirt by the brush.

"Cobb! Bring me those coolers," Rand ordered as he got down and worked the blade under the animal's hide.

Cobb moved around to the rear side fender. He grabbed the side railing, placed his right boot on top of the curved rubber of the mud and snow tire, and pulled himself up.

The two blue coolers were against the wheel well, next to the animal cage that was mostly covered by a tarpaulin.

Cobb leaned in to grab a handle on one of the pull-along coolers.

The cage rattled wildly as the creature inside screeched, fighting to get out.

Cobb jumped back away from the truck.

"Jesus, Cobb. Don't tell me you're afraid of that little thing?"

"Yeah, well, that little thing almost tore off my hand." Cobb showed his brother the deep scratches and the bite marks on his hand that he'd gotten when they'd first captured it and he had tried to get it into the cage.

"You'll heal. Quit your bellyaching."

"You know, Halsey. I don't think we should be doing this anymore."

Halsey glanced over at the puddle of puke at the base of the tree. "Lost your stomach for it, eh?"

"It's just not right."

"That so."

"Cobb! Get your ass over here," Rand yelled. He stood up and looked over at the truck, waiting impatiently. His bare forearms and the material on his shirt were slathered with blood, even though he'd rolled up his sleeves. The once-white painter's mask was speckled with crimson spots.

Halsey put his beer can on the tailgate. He got up on the back of the truck, grabbed both coolers, and tossed them down on the ground. "There! Take one and the shovel."

"Why do I always have to do the digging?" Cobb whined. "Why can't Rand ever take a turn?"

"Because he's the one that's good with a knife, and you're good with a shovel."

Cobb knew it was useless to argue. He grabbed a shovel out of the back of the truck and pulled one of the coolers behind him as he went over to where Rand was back to field dressing the big animal.

Halsey donned a respirator mask and put on cut-resistant gloves. He grabbed the kitchen axe from the tailgate. He brought the other cooler and headed over to where Rand was diligently working.

Cobb found a soft spot near the base of a pine tree and began digging a hole.

"And make it deep this time," Halsey said.

"Yeah, I heard you," Cobb replied, standing on the edge of the blade and scooping out a shovel full of dirt.

"Looks like there's quite a bit of meat on this one," Halsey said, standing over the dead animal and seeing how much meat Rand had already trimmed off the carcass.

"Oh, she's a plump one, that's for sure," Rand said, not bothering to look up as he sliced through the thick upper thigh.

Halsey got down on his knees and began to chop away.

11

Billy was clearing off a table when he saw Ralph Tillerman and Macy Givens come in. Ralph Tillerman always boasted that his favorite restaurant was the Porterville Steakhouse. He made a habit of eating there three times a week without fail, twice for lunch, and once when he would take his wife and four kids so they could take advantage of the family specials on Friday nights.

Usually for lunch, Ralph would bring one of his employees from the Food Mart with him—Dutch treat, of course—as he always drove.

Today, Ralph had asked his assistant manager, Macy Givens, to come and eat with him. Billy and Macy had been in the same grade and had dated a few times in their sophomore year but nothing serious. Macy was also Kit's best friend.

Billy hoped he might get a chance to talk with Macy, put a bug in her ear and see if she might talk to Kit and smooth things out between them.

Penny sat Ralph and Macy at a table by a window.

With people coming and going, Billy kept busy bussing and preparing tables. He kept one eye on the table by the window, hoping that Macy might excuse herself to go to the restroom and he could catch a quick word.

He purposely walked by as Penny was taking their order and smiled at Macy. "Hello, Macy. How're you?"

Macy glanced up. "Oh, hi Billy," but didn't say anymore and stared out the window, leaving Billy no choice but to keep walking. He stopped by the counter and was close enough that he could hear them talk.

"We're going to have the grilled bone steaks," Ralph said to Penny, not giving Macy the chance to decide for herself.

"But that's twenty ounces," Macy said with alarm. "I couldn't possibly eat that much."

"Believe me, it's the best thing you'll ever put in your mouth," he said with a smirk. "Once you've taken your first bite, you'll be surprised how much you can pack away," Ralph said from experience.

"If you like," Penny said, "I can ask Gordy to make it a smaller portion."

"Why do that?" Ralph interceded. "You can always get a doggy bag. Let me tell you, it's going to taste just as good, if not better, the next day. I kid you not."

"Okay, I'll go along with Ralph," Macy said.

"Believe me, you won't regret it."

Billy watched Penny walk over and clip the new ticket on the turnstile. He noticed a couple leaving. He grabbed his empty plastic tub and went over to the table. He collected their dirty dishes, cutlery, crumpled napkins, and half-filled beverage cups and put them in the carrier. He used a wet dishrag and wiped down the tabletop.

A five-dollar tip was tucked between the catsup bottle and saltshaker. Billy grabbed the bill. He reset the table with new napkins and cutlery and headed to the kitchen with the tub of dirty dishes.

Gordy called out that an order was up and Penny rushed over to collect the two freshly prepared plates of food.

As she passed by Billy, he discreetly slipped the fiver into her uniform pocket so later they could divvy the tips up between them.

"Thanks, Billy," Penny said, and shot him a smile.

He hustled into the back of the kitchen and placed the tub on the rinse counter where he'd left another tub that he had brought in a few minutes ago. It was always better to stay ahead of the game and not let the food get caked on the plates as later it just made it more difficult to get them clean.

He snatched the spray nozzle attached to a long hose and began rinsing off the plates one at a time before immersing them into a sink full of hot, sudsy water. He emptied the partially filled plastic beverage cups in another sink then tossed them into the soapy water, along with the cutlery. He quickly rinsed all the utensils and placed them on the drying rack.

In less than two minutes, he was back in the dining room.

Time enough for Ralph Tillerman's face to turn beet-red as he choked on his lunch.

"Oh my God, somebody help him," Macy screamed.

The other customers turned and stared with their forks in midair but nobody bothered to get up from their chairs.

Penny rushed over and stood behind Ralph's chair. "Ralph, stand up! I need you to get up, now!"

Ralph made an attempt to cough up his food but it only made him gag more. He leaned forward, grabbed his throat with one hand, and pushed up from the table with his other hand.

Penny kicked his chair aside and placed her arms around Ralph's chest. She made a fist with one hand and cupped it with the other, and with one inward thrust, rammed under his sternum.

A glob of meat the size of an apricot shot out of his mouth and sailed over Macy's head.

Everyone dropped their knives and forks and cheered, giving Penny a loud round of applause.

"Are you okay, Ralph?" Penny asked with genuine concern.

"Yes, that'll teach me to chew."

"You really scared me," Macy said.

"Sorry. Maybe we should get back to the store."

"Let me get you both some boxes," Penny said, and hurried to the counter.

Gordy stepped out of the kitchen when he heard everyone clapping, thinking it was his customers showing their appreciation for his culinary skills. But when he saw the strained look on Ralph Tillerman's face, he knew there had been a mishap and did an about-face back to his cooking station.

Penny came back with the carryout boxes but only Macy chose to bring her meal home as Ralph had lost his appetite. Ralph gave Penny the money for the bill and told her to keep the change.

Ralph and Macy got up from the table and walked out through the front door.

Billy walked up to Penny and patted her on the arm. "Wow, Penny, that was really something. Bet he gave you a monster tip."

"You think? Here's your half." Penny handed Billy a single bill.

"A buck! Are you serious, he gave you—"

But then he was interrupted when the front entrance door banged open.

Macy ran in yelling, "Somebody, please hurry! Ralph Tillerman's having a heart attack in the parking lot."

12

When Abel pulled his cruiser into the front parking lot of the Porterville Steakhouse, the paramedics had already covered Ralph Tillerman in hopes of discouraging the half a dozen people still meandering near the body. Abel noted that three of the townspeople were holding white take-home boxes.

Abel got out of his patrol car.

Margery Simmons and Blanche Mayberry turned as he approached and had guilty looks on their faces. Cindy Lambert slapped her husband's hand and Bernie put his cell phone away in his pocket.

Abel asked if anyone had actually seen Ralph Tillerman collapse and they all shook their heads.

"Then I suggest you all get in your cars and give the man some privacy."

The small group dispersed. They hurried over to their cars and left.

Abel opened the patrol car's rear door. Cooper was waking up from a nap on the backseat.

"Be a good time to stretch those legs," Abel said.

Cooper yawned, jumped down out of the car, and sauntered off toward the woods.

Abel knew just about everyone in town, Ralph being a casual acquaintance. He would often see Ralph working alongside the clerks whenever he shopped at the Food Mart. On occasion, Abel would see Ralph and his family at town picnics and special events. Ralph and his staff would often volunteer to barbeque and serve the food line.

But Ralph was what was referred to as a "walking time bomb." He was grossly overweight and whenever Abel saw Ralph at the supermarket, the man's face was always ruddy and his skin was clammy.

So it seemed reasonable that Ralph would walk out into the parking lot and drop dead from a heart attack, despite the fact that the dispatcher had relayed to Abel how Ralph had almost choked to death inside the restaurant while eating and was saved by Penny Styles after she performed the Heimlich maneuver on him.

"Hey, Bill," Abel said, addressing paramedic Bill Hastings, seating sideways in the passenger seat of the ambulance with the door open.

"Afternoon, Sheriff."

"You guys can take off. I've already called for the coroner's van."

"Sure. I'll get a report to your office later today."

"That'd be fine."

Bill closed his door and signaled to the other paramedic that they could leave. The ambulance crept out of the parking lot and turned onto the main highway.

Abel spotted Cassidy Muller, a grocery clerk from the Food Mart, standing at the restaurant's front entrance next to a brown Chevy Impala. She and Penny Sykes appeared to be consoling Macy Givens, who was staring down at the ground and had apparently been crying.

Penny had been the one that had called 911. She had given a thorough account of what happened to Gayle Becker who ran the Township Answering Service and had dispatched the police call to Abel and filled him in over the radio as he made his way to the scene. So there wasn't much that he didn't already know.

He thanked Penny and told her she could go back inside.

He spared Macy with only a few questions then told her she could go home. She said she would have to go back to work because as assistant manager it was now her responsibility to make sure everything ran smoothly at the supermarket until a new supervising manager was assigned.

Able knew she had high hopes of filling the position.

He watched Macy get in the front passenger seat of Cassidy's car and they drove away.

Even though it wasn't a crime scene, he still didn't want potential looky-loos showing up to sneak a peek at poor Ralph, so he moved his cruiser and partially blocked the driveway to dissuade anyone from coming into the parking lot until the body was removed.

Abel stepped aside when Bud arrived in his tow truck.

Five minutes later, a large, white hospital van veered into the parking lot. The driver parked next to the tow truck, turned off the engine, and got out.

Orderlies Ron Tully and Dave Rockford walked back to the rear of the van and opened the twin doors. When they pulled out the flat stretcher, the legs expanded down and the raised platform turned into a gurney on wheels. A black body bag was folded on top.

"Hey, Ron. Dave," Abel said.

Between their normal orderly duties at the Medical Center, Ron and Dave also filled in at the morgue.

"Jesus, isn't he the manager over at the Food Mart?" Ron said as soon as he uncovered Ralph Tillerman's body.

"That's right," Abel said.

"Damn," Dave said.

The two men pushed the gurney over so that it was parallel with Ralph's body then collapsed the legs so that the stretcher was flat on the ground. Ron took the body bag and shook it out. He pulled the zipper down the entire length of the bag and laid it out flat beside the dead man.

Ron raised Ralph's upper torso over the open bag while Dave lifted the dead man by both ankles and swung his feet in. Ron closed the zipper.

The men loaded the body bag onto the gurney and lifted it up to expand the legs.

They pushed the gurney to the rear of the emergency vehicle. The legs folded back up as they shoved the gurney into the back of the van.

Bud had finished hoisting Ralph's car up to the tow bar.

Abel watched as the tow truck followed the van out of the parking lot and each vehicle turned onto the highway, Bud going in the opposite direction.

He glanced around but didn't see Cooper anywhere.

"Coop! Time to go!"

The dog was nowhere to be seen.

Abel wondered if he had wandered behind the restaurant. He walked along the side of the building, went around the corner, and passed the dumpster.

The rear door was propped open with a mop bucket, so he walked right in.

He could hear Gordy yelling. "How the hell did *he* get in here?"

"I don't know. Must have snuck in."

Abel recognized Billy Boggs' voice.

"Did you leave the back door open again?"

"It's easier that way when I'm dumping the trash."

"What's going on?" Abel said as he stepped into the kitchen.

"Your damn dog, that's what!" Gordy growled.

The Alsatian was sitting on the floor, staring up at Billy.

"Coop, no begging." Abel saw a stack of dishes on a counter ready to be washed and a single plate with food still on it. "That wouldn't by any chance be Ralph Tillerman's meal?"

"Yeah, I believe so," Billy said. "Everyone else took theirs home."

"I'm going to need that for evidence. Could you put it in a box?"

"Sure thing, Sheriff."

Abel watched Billy as he grabbed a take-home box from a large stack on a shelf and scraped the food off the plate into the container and closed it up. Each box had the restaurant's distinct trademark and logo on the lid—an artist's rendition of a plump steak on a plate with the letters **PSH** shaped in a half-moon crest on the top.

"What, are you accusing me of something?" Gordy said.

"Just following procedure," Abel said, as Billy handed him the container.

"Hey, it's bad enough your dog's back here violating every health code in the book; now you're suggesting I gave Tillerman food poisoning?"

"No reason to get excited."

"Excited?" Gordy yelled. "That dog of yours better not shit in here."

"Well, on that note, I guess we'll be leaving. Come along, Coop." Abel gave the German shepherd some incentive and held the box under his nose.

Abel started back through the kitchen, Cooper trotting right behind. But when Abel happened to glance back over his shoulder, he saw the dog had stopped to sniff the bottom of the walk-in freezer door. "Coop, let's go."

Cooper pressed his nose to the floor and snorted like a pig.

"Hey, he better not be raising his leg," Gordy shouted.

"That's enough, boy. Let's go!" This time, Abel grabbed Cooper's collar and towed him out through the back. He made sure to kick the mop bucket out of the way so that door would close behind him. Certainly didn't want Cooper doubling back and getting into more trouble with Gordy and inciting a riot.

Abel let Cooper into the back of the cruiser.

He dug out his car keys and opened the trunk.

He slipped the take-home box inside into a large evidence bag and left it in the cargo compartment.

Abel got behind the wheel and glanced over at the back seat.

Cooper was already asleep.

13

Cobb Levitt was hot and sweaty from digging the hole then burying the carcass while Halsey and Rand sat on the tailgate, drinking beer. He hated being the youngest and always having to cow down to his older siblings. Even though he was almost as big as Halsey and had twenty pounds on Rand, he knew better than to rile his brothers as they always sided together. A few times he had made the mistake of getting into it with Rand and, like all the times before, Halsey stepped in and gave him a good beating.

So when Halsey turned off the main road and pulled up to the pump just outside the mini-store gas station, Cobb knew he'd be expected to go inside and pay for the gas.

"Fifty bucks should fill it up," Halsey said, sitting behind the wheel and shutting down the engine.

"I don't have any money," Cobb said.

"Didn't I just give you your cut from the other day?"

"Well, yeah, but I didn't think I was going to have to spend it on gas."

"What, you think you're riding for free?"

"I don't see Rand chipping in."

"That's because we're telling you," Rand piped in, relaxing in the backseat with Grover sitting beside him, the dog panting with drool hanging out of his mouth.

Cobb reached inside his trouser pocket and came up with three crumpled twenties.

"See, you got it," Halsey said.

As Cobb started to get out, Rand grabbed him by the shoulder.

"Here, take this and dump it."

Cobb turned and Rand shoved a wadded up shirt in his face that reeked of blood.

He jumped out of the truck and walked around the two gasoline pumps on the concrete island and headed for the front entrance of the mini-store.

A tall white trash bin was out front on the walkway in the front of the building.

He pushed the swinging door on the domed lid and shoved in Rand's shirt.

As he approached the entrance, the sliding glass doors glided open.

The air conditioning felt so good that he didn't think he would ever want to leave; especially as the compression pump had crapped out in the truck.

Danny Grimes was at the register and as soon as he saw Cobb, he slipped his magazine under the counter. "Hi there, Cobb. What can I do for you?"

"Give me fifty on…" Cobb paused to glance out the window. "Put that on pump number three."

"All right." Danny tapped a few buttons on the register.

Cobb looked down at the candy display and grabbed himself a Snickers bar. "And I'll take this."

He handed Danny the sixty dollars and got back his change. He tucked the candy bar in his shirt pocket, thanked the young man, and walked out of the store.

He happened to glance over and noticed that some blood from Rand's shirt had smeared onto the lid of the trash bin.

Cobb walked around the island and opened the passenger door on the truck. He was halfway in when Halsey said. "It ain't going to pump itself."

"But I just paid. Why can't Rand do it?"

"Because we're going to be too busy eating this," Rand said, leaning over the front seat and snatching Cobb's candy bar out of his pocket. He broke the bar in two and passed half to Halsey.

Halsey and Rand both grinned and took bites.

"You know, someday," Cobb said in a threatening tone.

"Someday what?" Halsey said.

"Yeah, little brother, someday what?" Rand grinned with chocolate on his teeth.

"Just forget it," Cobb said and slammed the door.

14

After Kit finished ringing up a customer, she went over to the gun section of the store to see if she could help her grandfather. She found him behind the glass display case, leaning over a crate with a battery-operated screwdriver. His hands were shaking and he was having trouble aligning the bit inside the screw head.

"Let me get that for you," Kit said.

Wiley Tanner knew his limitations and didn't even put up a fuss. "Sure, here you go," he said good-naturedly and handed Kit the power tool.

She went around the box and removed the screws holding the lid down. She took off the wood top and leaned it against the wall.

Six rifles were inside the crate, resting in well-padded individual foam inserts to ensure the firearms weren't damaged during transit.

"I've had a few calls for these Remington Model Sevens."

Kit noticed that the rifles were all the same type but not all of them looked similar as three were painted a camouflage green, the other three guns a subtle blue from the butt stocks to the tip of the muzzles

"Well, aren't they fancy," Kit said.

"Designer guns seem to be the rage."

"I wish you'd stop selling them."

"To tell you the truth, I've been given it some thought. When you get as old as me, you start looking at things differently."

"You're really considering it?"

"Well, when I decided to expand the store's inventory and sell firearms, I was a hunter myself. But as I got older, I guess I just lost the taste for it. Especially when people would come in and ask me why I wasn't carrying assault rifles and all those other ridiculous guns. What kind of hunter goes around killing deer with an AK-47? And I was damned if I'd be selling guns to some radical survivalist group just so they could take on the government. The hell with that."

"So why did you order these?" Kit asked.

"I don't know. Didn't want to disappoint my customers. But this will be the last time, I swear. I know how you and your mom hate guns."

"Well, it's not really fair to expect us to work here against our beliefs," Kit said.

"Oh? Don't tell me you and your mom are going to picket the store?"

"No, Grandpa," Kit said with a laugh. "Just hate to see all those poor animals out there being hunted down, that's all."

"Spoken like a true vegetarian."

15

Lucy Banks' favorite rock and roll band was currently playing. She had every song they had every recorded downloaded on her media player. At the moment, the front singer was belting out one of their biggest hits about her stormy relationship with one of her band members. Lucy especially liked the instrumental riff in the middle of the song and listened through her earbuds as she worked.

Being a cross-trained technician, she had been busy throughout the afternoon, performing blood tests in the laboratory and taking patients' x-rays across the hall.

Even though she was backed up with hospital requests, she knew it must be important for the sheriff to ask Dr. Turner if she could use her clout and bump up his evidence sample. Lucy always got a little excited whenever she got the opportunity to do something out of the realm of her normal duties, especially anything that involved criminology work.

She was careful not to let Dr. Turner's note fall off the plastic evidence bag and took out the red-tipped Q-tip. She took the applicator and rubbed the crust off onto a glass slide for a dried blood analysis.

Another song came on that she loved, a heartfelt ballad about personal loss. She increased the volume on her earbuds.

Lucy carried the slide over to the high-power microscope and positioned it under the revolving nosepiece. She turned on the lamp so the light would shine up through the diaphragm and illuminate the brittle blood sample.

But as she lowered her head to peer in the eyepiece, a hand grabbed her shoulder.

Lucy jerked up and turned. She pulled out her earbuds and switched off her media player.

"Whoa, aren't we a little jumpy," Ron Tully said with a big grin on his face.

"How many times do I have to tell to quick sneaking up on me like that?" Lucy snapped.

"Luce, come on, dial it down a notch."

Lucy gave him a scowl.

"Want to come see who we just brought in?" Ron asked.

"Why, who do you have?"

"Would you believe, Ralph Tillerman?"

"Are you serious?"

"Serious as a heart attack. Well, I guess that wasn't very nice, seeing as he died from a heart attack."

"Can I see him?"

"Yes, you may," Ron said.

They walked out of the lab and crossed the hall to the morgue.

"Here," Ron said, handing Lucy a small jar of Vicks Vaporub.

Lucy knew the drill and unscrewed the lid. She used the tip of her finger and dabbed some of the mentholated topical ointment under her nose to mask the putrid smell of rotting flesh that was always prevalent inside the morgue no matter how many times the room was cleaned with disinfectants and deodorizers. She closed the jar and handed it back.

Before Ron could use his key, the door swung open. Dave Rockford shoved a gurney out through the doorway. "Make a hole!"

Lucy and Ron jumped out of his way.

"Got a call that we're needed upstairs," Dave said as he pushed the gurney toward the exit door. He stopped for a moment, opened up the control box, and turned off the switch to deactivate the emergency alarm.

He pushed open the door and looked over his shoulder as he steered the gurney outside. "Mine turning that back on? I'll come back in through the front way once I've put this back in the van and meet you topside."

"Sure thing, Davy."

As soon as the door closed behind Dave, Ron went over and turned the switch back on. He looked at Lucy. "Come in for a quick peek then I've got to get back up there."

Lucy didn't think of herself as a terrible person for wanting to go into the morgue and see dead people.

Everyone did it. Look at all those mourners that lined up at funerals and wakes so they could view their beloved in an open casket.

She never considered it morbid curiosity.

Going into the morgue was like being part of the elite; entering a place reserved only for morticians and medical examiners.

As soon as they stepped inside the room, Lucy could feel the drop in temperature as the refrigeration units used to contain the corpses were all set for forty degrees Fahrenheit to slow down the rate of decomposition. Every time a door was opened, it would chill the air.

Ralph Tillerman was lying on the stainless steel autopsy table. A white sheet was draped over his body. Lucy knew that he was naked beneath the sheet as there was a clear bag containing his clothes by his feet. His right foot was sticking out from under the sheet. A cardboard toe tag was tied to his big toe.

Usually when dead people were brought in, their facial expressions were relaxed and they looked peaceful.

Ralph Tillerman's facial expression was anything but. He looked like he'd been in excruciating pain. His eyes were still open and his mouth was agape like he'd died midway into a scream. His skin was blue, the same shade as a Smurf.

A loud disgusting noise sounded under the sheet.

"Oh God," Ron said, pinching his nostrils.

"Did he just fart?" Lucy asked, trying to keep from laughing.

"What the hell did this guy eat?" Ron waved his hand in the air. "Man, that's bad! Let's get out of here."

They rushed out of the room like a couple of giddy children, scampering away down the hall after peeking in on their parents having a morning tryst.

Ron gave Lucy a quick kiss on the lips and ran for the stairwell.

Lucy went back inside the laboratory. She sat on the stool in front of the microscope and examined the dried blood sample on the slide. She compared the white blood cells with every picture in her blood cell biochemistry book that she kept on her desk, which referenced both human and animal types, but couldn't come up with an exact match.

She picked up the Q-tip and studied the blood on the cotton.

"So if you're not in the book, then what are you?"

16

"Knock knock," Abel said, standing casually in the doorway of Kate's office.

"Oh, hello," Kate replied. She shuffled some papers on her desk, put them in a single stack, and placed the pile in her in-coming box. "I guess this can wait until tomorrow." She pushed her chair back and stared up at Abel.

"You look tired," he said.

"I am," she replied.

Cooper wandered into the office. He came around the desk and sat down beside Kate's chair.

Kate leaned down and kissed the dog on the dome of his head.

Cooper reciprocated and licked her face.

"Well, that was refreshing," she said with a smile.

"Maybe you two would like to be alone."

Kate put her arm around Cooper's shoulders and looked him in the eyes. "I think the sheriff's a little jealous, what do you think?"

Cooper responded with a forceful bark.

"That's enough out of you, Deputy." Abel grabbed Kate's coat off the hanger on the back of the door. He held the jacket out as she got up from her desk and walked over. She turned her back and Abel guided her arms into the sleeves. She pulled the jacket up around her shoulders and zipped up the front.

Abel waited for Kate and Cooper to come out then flicked off the light and shut the door.

As they headed down the corridor, Abel saw Grant and Kit coming their way.

"Evening," Abel greeted.

"Abel. Dr. Turner," Grant replied. "How's Bess doing?"

"She's doing much better," Kate said. "She's awake. If all goes well, we should be releasing her in a day or two."

"That's great to hear. Thank you."

"You're more than welcome, Grant."

"Well, we better—"

A car alarm blared in the parking lot.

Abel went over to a window that overlooked the parking lot below.

"Aren't those floodlights on a timer?" he asked.

"I believe they're set to go on once the sun goes down," Kate said.

"Well, they haven't. It's pretty dark down there. I'm going down and see what triggered that alarm."

Vera Rivers stepped away from the nursing station and came to the window. "I believe that's my car making all that racket. It's a white Toyota Camry. Here's my fob." She handed Abel the remote control.

"I'll be right back."

"I'm coming with you," Grant said.

"Sure. Kate, keep Cooper with you."

"Okay." Kate held onto the Alsatian's collar as the two men walked away.

Abel and Grant took the front stairs and went out through the lobby.

The high-pitched car alarm was ear-splitting as they rounded the building.

Abel pointed the fob at Vera's car and pushed the button.

The alarm made a blip sound and went silent.

It was pitch dark. Abel counted maybe ten cars in the lot.

"Over here," Grant said.

Abel made his way over to where Grant was standing. His boot came down and crunched over broken glass. He took his flashlight off his belt and shined the light up at the overhead floodlight. The lamp had been smashed out.

"Must have used this," Grant said. He leaned down and picked up a big rock off the asphalt.

"Would explain the other lights."

They heard a loud crash and breaking glass.

"What the hell was that?" Abel said, swinging the flashlight in the direction of the sound.

A large shape darted behind a hedgerow that separated the reserved spaces from the rest of the public parking.

"Who's out there?" Abel yelled.

Abel shined his light on the back of a truck. The rear cab window was busted out.

"That's my truck," Grant said. He approached the vehicle and looked inside the cab. The 40-pound bear trap that he had confiscated off the mountain, and left on the bed, was now lying on the seat inside the cab.

"Well, that's weird," Abel said.

"I think I know who did this," Grant said.

"Who?"

"Halsey Levitt. I'm pretty sure that's his trap."

"Then why didn't he just take it?"

"I don't know; maybe it's a message to back off."

"Well, if he threatens you, just—"

There was another crash, this time it was on the other side of the closely spaced shrubs.

Abel found a walkthrough between the bushes and shined his flashlight around until the beam landed on his cruiser.

"What happened to your car?" Grant asked as they walked over to investigate.

The trunk was dented and the lid had been pried open.

Abel shined the light inside the cargo compartment.

"Anything taken?" Grant asked.

"Everything looks accounted for," Abel said. "No, wait. There is something missing."

"What's that, one of your guns?"

"No, a take-home box from the steakhouse."

"Someone broke into your trunk to steal some food?"

"It contained the meal Ralph Tillerman was having before his heart attack. I was keeping it as evidence."

"Who would want that?"

"I have my suspicions."

"Mind sharing?"

"Gordy Oxman.

"You think he has something to hide?"

"Well, he wasn't too thrilled when I told him I wanted to take Tillerman's meal with me."

"You think he wrecked my truck to throw us off?" Grant said.

"It's a good possibility."

17

Bud Tinker stood under the hoist and finished tightening the oil plug on Jamie Masterson's old Plymouth. The car was more of a relic than a classic but ran like a top because Jamie always brought it in for regular oil changes and tune-ups like Bud recommended to all of his customers. Being the only real mechanic in town, it wasn't unusual for him to stay late into the night fixing cars in the station's bay.

He unhooked the droplight from the car's frame, went over to the hydraulic lever, and lowered the car lift. He walked around to the front of the Plymouth and raised the hood.

A funnel and six cans of motor oil were waiting on the workbench.

A welcoming breeze blew into the garage through the opening under the raised roll-up door. It felt so good Bud decided to take a break and go outside to enjoy the night air.

He picked up a rag and wiped the grease from his hands.

As he walked outside, he was greeted by the sound of cicadas and tiny flying moths drawn to the light above the office door. He strolled over and made sure he had put the padlocks on the pumps as he was officially closed to customers. He'd even turned off the Texaco sign so no one would think he was open for business.

The mountain air felt good on his face and he could smell the pine forest across the road.

He turned and was about to go back inside and put oil in Jamie's Plymouth when he thought he heard something around back in the wrecking yard. Still worrying his hands with the rag, Bud walked down the side of the garage to the cyclone fence.

The gate was open. He could have sworn he'd closed it, but lately he had been getting more forgetful.

Only a couple of days ago, Nelly Coates had come in with a flat right front tire which should have been easy enough. Bud had grabbed a spray bottle filled with soapy water and quickly found the leak. Normally, he would use a special tool and put a rubber plug in the tire, but Nelly's tires had inner tubes.

So he had to jack up her car and remove the tire. He put it on a tire changer then separated the tire from the rim and took out the tube. He saw the puncture right away and glued on a patch. After he replaced the tire back on the rim, he slapped the tire back on the car and used a pneumatic wrench to tighten the lug nuts.

He remembered Nelly thanking him as she got in her car and started to drive away.

That's when he realized he had forgotten to put on her hubcap and two of the lug nuts that were lying inside. Luckily, she had heard him yell before she got to the main road. He remembered apologizing as he ran over with the lug nuts, hubcap, and a lug wrench. It took him less than a minute to finish up but when he stood and looked at Nelly through the side window, he could tell that she wasn't happy by the look she gave him.

He heard a sound like metal grinding against metal coming from inside the yard.

He stepped through the gate and walked cautiously between the ruined cars. He had purposely lined them up in three rows. Last time he counted, there were over a hundred cars and trucks, most of them dismantled to some degree as Bud let customers come in to salvage automobile parts. Some of the cars had their hoods up, left open from the last person rummaging through the engines.

He walked by the forklift he used to move the cars as none of them ran anymore.

The equipment was powerful enough that he could drop the forks down on the car roofs and flatten the vehicles so he could stack them two or three high.

He heard another screech of metal.

"Hello? Who's back here?"

Bud waited for someone to answer but instead heard a sharp grinding noise.

He wished he'd thought to bring along a flashlight. It was so dark he couldn't see twenty feet in front of him.

After a few more steps, he realized he was standing next to the Tanner's Volvo that he had recently brought in.

He glanced up at the outline of crushed cars on the heaped row contrasted against the night sky.

That's when he saw the hulking figure standing up there.

"Hey, get the hell down from there before you break your fool neck! You're trespassing on private property!"

The shape bent down.

Bud heard that grinding noise again.

The figure rose slowly, holding a large object over its head. "I'm warning you…get the hell out of my—"

18

"See you tomorrow, Billy," Penny said. She had her coat on and was slipping the strap of her purse over her shoulder.

"Night, Penny," Billy replied, stacking a pot he had just cleaned onto a shelf. He waved as Penny walked past and went out the back door.

It had been a busy shift and the tips hadn't been half bad. Working in a restaurant was a hard way to make a living; especially with the measly salary Gordy was paying him. Billy doubted if he was even getting state minimum wage. So he was always appreciative when Penny shared her tips with him.

Out of curiosity one night, when Penny was divvying the money, Billy asked her how the custom started. She explained that the word *tip* was actually an acronym for To Insure Promptness, and years ago, patrons would pay money up front so the servers would know which customers were the big tippers and give them extra attention.

Over time, the dining experience changed and people chose to wait until after their meal before dispensing gratuity, which meant that if servers didn't want to jeopardize receiving a lavish tip, they would have to give everyone the same degree of personal service.

Penny didn't care one way or the other. She knew just about everyone that came into the steakhouse; those that were courteous and generous, the ones that complained about the silliest things and stiffed her.

Billy knew Penny was the kind of person that always stepped up her game, no matter what. Even though she was five years older than him, Billy had to admit that he had a bit of a crush on her. Sure, he liked Kit and all, but sometimes she wasn't always so nice to him. At least, Penny was consistent even though he knew deep down they were just friends.

He grabbed his coat and walked passed Gordy's office. The door was open. Gordy was sitting at his desk, adding up receipts on a calculator.

"I'm leaving," Billy said.

Gordy grunted and kept tapping on the keys.

Billy went through the back of the kitchen and out the rear door.

He looked up at the dark clouds cumulated in the night sky. There was a steady breeze coming down from the mountain, a good indicator that rain was on the way.

Like most nights when he got off of work, there were only the two vehicles in the rear parking lot—Billy's Honda and Gordy's truck.

Billy got into his car. It was freezing so he rubbed his hands together. He dug in his coat pocket, took out his car key, and put it in the ignition. He turned the key and the engine groaned for a moment then started right up. The car shook slightly from the rough idle, as the engine was overdue for a tune-up. Once the engine warmed up, the car would run smoother.

Billy gave it a couple minutes then put the car into gear and pulled out of his parking spot. He drove behind the restaurant and headed for the back street that eventually connected with the main road.

He was almost ready to turn when the engine sputtered and the car came to a shuddering stop.

"Damn you," he swore. He turned the ignition key to restart the car. The starter motor labored to turn over the engine. Billy kept pumping the gas pedal with his right foot and held the key in the forward position. He feared he was putting a strain on the battery, as the system seemed to be winding down. The carburetor was flooded. There was nothing for him to do but wait for the fuel to settle and any air vapors to dissipate.

Billy switched off the ignition and turned off the headlights so as not to further run down the battery. It was cold, so he zipped his jacket up all the way, and settled back in his seat.

He spotted headlights coming down the main road. A truck pulled into the front parking lot of the steakhouse then drove around the side and pulled up by the back door under the floodlight.

It was the Levitt's truck.

Halsey climbed out of the driver's side. Rand got out on the passenger side and they both walked to the back of the truck. Halsey lowered the tailgate.

Gordy came out the back door and held it open.

The men talked for a moment but Billy had no idea what they were saying as they were too far away.

There were no streetlights where he'd stalled out and it was pretty dark, so he doubted if they knew he was even watching but he ducked down in his seat anyway.

Rand pulled a large ice chest out of the back of the truck and put it on the ground. Then he reached up and retrieved a second cooler.

Gordy motioned them in.

The Levitt brothers each grabbed a cooler on wheels. Halsey went in first, followed by Rand. Gordy scanned the parking lot but didn't happen to look Billy's way.

Billy watched Gordy go inside and close the door behind him.

He tried the car again.

This time, it fired right up.

He slipped the car into gear and sped off.

19

Abel filled his travel cup with coffee from the pot on the stove. He was dressed for work and getting ready to leave.

Cooper was by the back door, raring to go.

Kate strolled into the kitchen. She was wearing one of Abel's shirts, a pair of black feminine briefs, and was barefoot. She poured herself a cup of coffee and sat down at the kitchen table.

"You know, Abel. People are going to start talking."

"What makes you think they're not already?"

"Knowing this town, you're probably right."

"So what do you suggest we do?"

"I don't know," Kate said and took a sip of her coffee.

"So you're putting it back in my lap?"

"Well, I do trust your judgment. You being the sheriff, and all."

"So what you're saying is, sharing a bed and wearing one of my favorite shirts isn't enough?"

"It's a start."

"Next you'll be trying to steal my dog."

"Already have." Kate patted the side of the chair. Cooper came running over and put his head on Kate's lap. She rewarded him with good neck rub.

"I best be going."

"Where you off to?"

"Well, I thought I might do something about that dented-up trunk. Don't want folks thinking I'm a bad driver. I'm the one that's supposed to be setting the example around here. Thought I'd swing by Bud's. If I recollect right, he has the same model Crown Victoria in his yard. Maybe I can get him to swap trunks."

Abel walked over and gave Kate a kiss.

"Well, thank you, Sheriff."

"You're much obliged." Abel grabbed his Stetson off the hook on the wall and squared his hat on his head.

He opened the back door and whistled for Cooper to come.

The Alsatian rolled his eyes up at Kate.

"You best be going," Kate said, doing a spot on impression of Abel.

Cooper darted out of the kitchen and beat Abel to the cruiser.

It was only a ten-minute drive over to the Texaco station.

When Abel pulled up to the pumps, he was surprised to see they were padlocked and the rollup door was raised all the way up. Normally, Bud would always get the station ready for business and anyone wanting gas first before opening the bay doors on the garage.

Something didn't seem right.

Abel climbed out of the car and let Cooper out. The dog immediately ran around the side of the building.

He walked over to the office and tried the door. It was locked. He went inside the garage and looked around.

"Bud, you in here?"

Abel could hear Cooper barking around back, so he went outside, and walked back to the wrecking yard.

The gate was wide open.

Bud had arranged most of the cars and trucks side by side so that it was easier for salvagers to access under the hoods and dismantle parts. The vehicles that had already been picked over were stacked two to three cars high in two separate rows along with other junk.

Cooper continued to bark, so Abel followed the sound.

He spotted his dog about fifty feet away, standing next to a body lying on the ground. Abel could see the bottoms of the boots, and as he got closer, he could read BUD on the nametag on the mechanic coveralls.

"Ah, Jesus," Abel said. He'd seen victims of gruesome murders and horrendous car wrecks while he'd been sheriff, but he had never seen anything as horrific as what he was witnessing now.

A car engine was partially embedded in the ground...

...in the same exact spot where Bud's head should have been.

Judging by the expansive halo of crimson gore, Abel figured the engine must have toppled down from a height of fifteen feet and pulverized Bud's skull.

The instrument of death was a short block, most likely a 302, which had to weigh somewhere in the vicinity of 300 pounds.

Abel looked down and saw Cooper licking something up from the ground.

"Oh my God, will you stop! That's disgusting!" Abel marched over to pull Cooper away from whatever it was he was eating, and in doing so, could hear his boots crunching over tiny pieces of bone fragments.

He grabbed Cooper by the collar, led him back to the cruiser, and put the dog in the back seat. He went round to the back of the car and opened the trunk. He took out his camera and a folded packet containing a sheet of plastic to cover Bud's body.

Abel used the radio in the cruiser and called it in. He told Gayle at the answering service to contact the hospital and have Ron and Dave come out to the wrecking yard with the coroner's van.

He left Cooper in the back of the car with the windows lowered enough to give him a cross breeze of air and went back to photograph the scene of the accident.

Bud Tinker had been a good friend and Abel was surely going to miss him.

It seemed such a strange way for him to die.

If there was ever a time he wished his office could afford a forensic photographer, this was it. Taking photos of Bud's body hadn't been so bad, but when it came to photographing the blood-splattered engine block and surrounding ground, Abel found it difficult to look through the viewfinder. He held the camera out at arms-length and snapped off a few pictures.

He looked up at the cars on the top. There were doors, fenders, along with other scrap material piled on the roofs. The dilapidated autos were tiered three high, the vehicles on the bottom compressed from the weight of the others on top. Seeing as the engine had fallen from up there, Abel knew he would have to climb up and take some more pictures to complete his report.

Slipping his camera into his coat pocket, he grabbed the window frame of the bottom wreck, and gave it a shake to see if anything would become dislodged from up above and come crashing down on his head. Nothing came loose.

He started to climb up using whatever handhold was available, careful not to cut his hands on any jagged metal or broken glass. He stepped up on the edge of a car seat, as the door was missing, and managed to pull himself up onto the roof of a rusted-out Ford Mustang.

He had to watch out that he didn't slip and fall off so he didn't stand up all the way and glanced down.

The hood of the car had been removed and the engine was missing.

He could see where the engine mounts had been snapped off.

There was no way this was an accident.

20

Billy hadn't slept well the night before as he couldn't stop thinking of Kit and the way she had given him the brush-off the other morning. He decided on a fast breakfast of cereal, which turned out to be a disaster as two bites in he realized the milk had gone bad even though it hadn't reached the expiration date. When he shook the carton, he could hear the curdled chunks sloshing around inside. He dumped the rancid milk into the sink and rinsed out the carton so that it wouldn't smell up the kitchen.

He hoped it wasn't a preamble to how the rest of his day was going to turn out.

He stopped for gas at the convenient store as they had the lowest prices and put in ten dollars worth. There were only a couple cars parked outside the front entrance of the Porterville Hardware and Hunting Supply.

Billy got out of his car and went inside.

Wiley Tanner was talking with a customer, something to do with plumbing supplies as they were standing in that section. Wiley paused for a moment and glanced over at Billy as he strolled down an aisle. He gave Billy a nod hello and went back to helping his customer. Even though Billy had never had a real conversation with the old man other than brief greetings, Wiley Tanner was always civil and never seemed to hold any animosity towards him.

Mrs. Tanner, Kit's mother, was another story.

Billy could sense the woman didn't care for him. Not that he had ever done anything to displease her other than be fond of her daughter. Whenever possible, Billy stayed clear of her. He knew he wouldn't have to worry about their paths crossing today, as she was still laid up in the hospital for which he felt both relieved and guilty at the same time.

He spotted Kit stocking a shelf with cleaning supplies and walked over.

"Hi there," Billy said.

Kit turned around, holding a detergent bottle in her hand. "Oh, hi Billy."

"Just thought I'd see how you were doing?"

"I'm okay."

"How's your mother?"

"She's doing better."

"That's good."

"You know, Billy. I'm really sorry, I shouldn't have been so rude to you."

"I get it. You were just worried about your mom."

"Then, you're not mad at me?" Kit asked.

"Heck no. I thought you were mad at me."

"Maybe I was, but not—"

"Kit! Can you come over here?" Wiley Tanner hollered from the other side of the store.

"Be right there!" Kit answered. "Don't go yet," she said to Billy. "I'll be right back."

Billy watched her go down the aisle and disappear around the corner.

He glanced over his shoulder while he waited and saw the office door was open.

Kit's purse was on the desk.

Billy thought about what Halsey had said to him, threatening to hurt Kit if he didn't get him a copy of the store's key.

Now seemed the perfect opportunity.

He checked to make sure Kit wasn't heading back and snuck into the office.

There was a set of keys in Kit's purse. Billy had no idea which one fit the back door of the store. Then he saw a single key attached to a small elastic lanyard, the type that would fit around someone's wrist. That had to be it. He took out the key and slipped it inside his pocket.

When he came out of the office, he could hear Kit and Wiley still talking with the customer on the other side of the aisles.

He quickly made his way over to the key-making machine. He knew how to operate the equipment as he had used it before. He inserted the store key into a slot then grabbed a key blank and placed it into the machine. He started up the motor, thankful that it wasn't too loud, and made the proper cuts. As soon as he was through, he took out the keys and shut off the machine.

Billy couldn't hear the voices anymore from across the store.

He rushed over, ducked inside the office, and dropped Kit's store key inside her purse. When he came out, Kit was just turning the corner and coming down the aisle.

"Was that you running the key-making machine?" she asked.

"Uh, yeah."

"Aren't you the sneaky one?"

"What?" Billy replied nervously.

"Cough it up."

"Cough what up?"

"That'll be one dollar. I'd be more than glad to let you have it for free, but it is my grandfather's store."

"Oh, sure." Billy reached in his back pocket, pulled out his slim wallet, and fished out a dollar bill.

"So, what's the key for?" Kit asked suspiciously.

"A spare for my house," Billy lied. "I thought it would be a good idea to hide one outside, just in case I ever lost my other one."

"Sure that's the reason?"

"What do you mean?"

"How do I know it's not for someone else?"

Billy could feel himself starting to sweat.

"Like that waitress you work with. What's her name? Penny?"

Bill let out a laugh and hoped it didn't sound too forced. "That's silly. Penny's way too old for me."

Kit gave him the evil stare.

"Uh, I better go or I'm going to be late for work." Billy glanced around to see if anyone was watching them then gave Kit a quick kiss, hoping she wouldn't object.

Her face brightened and she even smiled.

Billy smiled back at her as he left.

He went outside and sat in his car.

He'd never felt more ashamed. Not only had he deceived Kit, he was about to put her grandfather's store in jeopardy.

Could the day get any crappier?

21

Danny Grimes hated working swing shift at the convenience store gas station but they were shorthanded so he had no choice. He was having trouble adjusting to the weird hours. Getting off at midnight, there wasn't much to do but go straight home as everything was closed. If he tried going to bed right away, he only tossed and turned because he would be too amped-up with a sugar rush from the frequent helpings at the soda dispenser; but then it was impossible to get a decent eight-hours sleep before going to work as the outside noises would always keep him awake.

He looked up at the clock behind the register and saw that it was only seven o'clock and he had five more hours before his shift was up. He heard the pattering of rain on the glass front of the store. The weather forecast on the news said they could expect a heavy storm.

The rainfall intensified. Danny could hear the downpour pelting the roof of his car and the asphalt of the parking lot outside. It was really coming down.

In a way, he was glad the weather was bad because it meant that there would be fewer customers, if any, wanting to venture out in the storm unless they were some fool having a nicotine fit and needed a pack of smokes or had run out of beer.

One of the perks working alone was he could help himself to whatever he wanted as long as he covered his tracks. Whenever he wanted a soda or a snack, Danny would reach under the counter and turn off the surveillance recorder so he wouldn't be caught on tape. It was a trick he'd taught the clerks on the other two shifts and so far their boss hadn't been any wiser.

Danny figured the only time the owner would bother looking at the tape was in the event of a robbery or some other emergency, and so far, neither had happened since he'd been working there.

He was feeling hungry and had a craving for some nachos. A big gulp of root beer would be good too.

Danny glanced around casually to make sure there was no one outside. He leaned on the counter and slyly slid his hand down and hit the stop button on the recorder.

He grabbed an empty 22-ounce plastic cup out of a stack, put it under the spout of the carbonated beverage machine, and filled it up to the rim with frothy root beer. He put a handful of tortilla chips in a disposable paper food tray then pumped the handle on the nacho cheese dispenser and poured the thick, yellow goop onto the chips. He added some sliced jalapenos to spice it up and scooped a cheesy chip into his mouth.

Danny was halfway done with his snack when he saw something wiggling in the gooey cheese. He used his finger to pick it out.

He scrunched up his face disgustedly when he realized it was a maggot.

"Aw, jeez!" He threw the serving tray down. The contents spilled out and more maggots went squirming onto the countertop.

He opened the lid on the nacho machine. There were so many maggots that it looked like someone had dumped rice in with the melted cheese. He couldn't remember the last time anyone had bothered to clean the machine.

He could feel the maggots moving about in his stomach, or so his mind tried to convince him, and truly believed he was going to die of food poisoning.

Danny ran out from behind the counter and dashed back to the restroom. He flung open the door, dropped to his knees, and threw up in the toilet that stunk from the last user, the smell so putrid that he hurled again. He leaned over the bowl with both hands on the toilet seat, sweat dripping from his forehead.

He wiped his mouth with the back of his hand and got up slowly. He turned on the cold-water tap, doused his face, and drank some water to get the bad taste out of his mouth.

That's when he heard the *ding*, which meant that the front doors had automatically opened. He glanced in the mirror. His face was pale and he looked sickly—like he had just puked. He staggered out of the restroom and shuffled over to the register.

The doors were still open. Heavy rain was blowing in, sopping the floor.

Danny could see a tall figure standing outside in the pouring rain. "Hey, get in here!" he yelled. "You're getting the place soaked!"

The white trash bin soared into the store and crashed onto the floor. The lid flew off and the contents spilled out. Danny saw a bloody shirt among the strewn paper cups and bags.

Danny heard a mighty roar and looked up.

The overhead fluorescent lights flickered off and came back on again, giving Danny a short-lived glimpse as the huge beast charged through the doorway at the exact moment the electricity went out and the store was cast into darkness.

22

Abel was doing his nightly patrol on the outskirts of town when he noticed there were no lights on at the 24-hour convenience store gas station.

He pulled into the front parking lot and kept his headlights on so they would shine inside the store. The automatic doors had apparently locked open when the power went out. There were puddles on the floor and at the rate the wind was blowing in the rain, the owner could expect some losses from water damage.

Abel opened his door and climbed out of the police cruiser in the pouring rain. He pulled the hood of his orange rain poncho tightly over his head. He glanced in at Cooper on the back seat. The dog was awake and sitting up but showed no interest in going out in the deluge. Instead, he slowly turned around three times then curled up on the seat.

"Hope you're warm enough," Abel said jokingly. He pushed the door closed and walked toward the front entrance of the store.

"Hello! Anyone inside?" Even though there was a fair amount of light shining in from the cruiser's headlamps, Abel still took out his flashlight and turned it on.

He saw a cylindrical trash bin on its side on the floor. The lid was a couple of feet away. Leaves and lightweight debris were blowing about the store.

Abel saw a balled-up shirt on the floor, covered with blood. He reached behind the counter, grabbed a plastic bag, and placed the grimy shirt inside as evidence. He shined his flashlight down an aisle stocked with canned goods and boxes of dried food.

There was so much blood on the linoleum that it looked like someone had dipped a heavy-duty wet mop into a bucket of blood and then dragged it down the aisle floor.

The trail of gore led back to the restroom.

Abel drew his revolver. He held his flashlight under the barrel of his gun and stepped toward the restroom door, careful not to step in the blood.

"Anyone back here?" he called out.

He heard a noise inside the washroom.

Abel pointed his flashlight at the door handle. He reached down, turned the knob, and edged the door open. He shined the light through the narrow opening.

All he could see was a lot of red.

An animal growled and slammed into the door, pinning Abel's hand. He dropped the flashlight and tried to wrench his hand free. The door burst open and a large shadowy figure shoved him out of the way into a row of shelves. The display collapsed and he fell through. Cartons of merchandise fell on top of him as he toppled to the floor.

He turned and caught a fleeting glimpse of the thing as it ran out of the store and disappeared into the pouring rain. He had no idea what it was, only that it had been incredibly strong and had steamrolled him like a bull. The assault had happened so unexpectedly he'd dropped his gun. He found his service revolver under a pile of smashed cereal boxes.

He could hear Cooper barking fitfully in the police cruiser.

He got up, approached the restroom, and slowly opened the door. A large chunk of porcelain had been broken off the edge of the sink and the mirror was dripping wet, splattered with viscera slime.

A pathetic, bloody heap was wedged between the toilet and the wall.

Abel thought it might be Danny Grimes but there was so much physical trauma, he couldn't be certain.

23

When the second floor went black, Kate waited patiently for the backup generators to kick on. The restored power was minimal, enough to drive the emergency medical equipment and the widely spaced overhead lighting.

Fortunately, there were only three patients occupying the hospital rooms: Bess Tanner, who was recovering nicely; Elma Brightly, a septuagenarian suffering from congestive heart failure; and teenage Mitch Brown, his right leg in a complete cast from his hip down to his toes and suspended in a sling, after falling off the roof while helping his father replace a spark arrestor on their chimney.

"I better check on Elma," Vera Rivers said as she got up from behind her desk at the nursing station.

"While you're doing that, I'll make sure Mitch and Bess are all right." Kate walked over to the teenager's room. The young man was fast asleep and was unaware that there had been a temporary power outage. Kate could see where his well-wishing friends had signed their names and doodled on his cast. He wasn't due for any medicine for another two hours so she let him sleep and left the door half-closed.

Bess, on the other hand, was wide-awake and sitting up in bed, her left arm in a cast. Heavy jellybean-size raindrops were beating on her window. "Sounds like we're in for quite a storm," she said when Kate came into her room.

"That's what everyone's saying," Kate said. "How's the arm? Any pain?"

"Not at the moment." Bess smiled and pressed the push-button on her pain relief pump.

"Any headaches?"

"No."

"That's good. Your brain scan appears normal and there is no sign of swelling. Can I bring you anything?"

"No, I'm fine. Has Grant or Kit come by?"

"I haven't seen them. But don't worry; I'll be discharging you tomorrow."

"That's good. I'll need to get back, help out at the store."

"You should take a few days to rest up."

"But Wiley can't—"

"Doctor's orders!" Kate said firmly but friendly. "At least give it a day or two."

"All right, if you insist," Bess said, her eyes drooping as the soothing pain medication took effect.

"I'll check on you a little later," Kate said but doubted if the woman heard her as she had already drifted off to sleep. She returned to the nursing station where Vera was already at her desk, doing her evening check off on her computer.

"Looks like it's going to be a quiet one," Kate said.

Vera looked up at Kate. "That's all right by me," and resumed typing on her keyboard.

They heard footsteps and looked down the hall. Abel had just come through the door that led to the stairwell. He was wearing an orange poncho and looked like he had been out in the storm. Cooper on the other hand was dry as a bone as he pranced alongside the sheriff.

"You're a little early," Kate said, thinking he was here to pick her up.

"Brought in Danny Grimes," Abel said.

"Where is he? Is he hurt?" Kate asked.

"No, he's dead."

"How?"

"He was attacked by some animal. It came at me but it happened so fast I didn't get a good look at it. Ron and Dave just dropped his body off downstairs in the morgue."

"Oh, before I forget. Lucy brought this up, said it was for you." Vera snatched the small evidence bag from her desk that contained the blood sample taken from the front bumper of Bess Tanner's Volvo and handed it to Abel.

A questioning look came over Abel's face when he looked at the attached Post-it note.

"What's wrong?" Kate asked.

"Lucy says the sample is unidentifiable."

"Maybe there wasn't enough for her to analyze."

"Maybe." Abel walked over to the red biomedical waste disposal can by the nursing station, stepped on the floor pedal, and when the lid popped open, he tossed in the evidence bag.

Cooper sauntered over and gave the can a sniff.

"Do you think he's hungry?" Kate asked.

"Tell me a time when he's not."

"Come on, Coop. I'll set you up with something in my office." Kate patted her thigh and started down the hall, Cooper trotting at her side. She wasn't gone for more than a minute when she returned to the nursing station.

"What'd you give him?" Abel asked.

"A ham and cheese sandwich from the vending machine."

"You keep that up he'll be turning his nose up every time I put out his kibble."

"What's that saying? The best way to a dog's heart is through his stomach."

"I believe that's *to a man's heart*," Abel said.

"Same difference."

***

Lucy tapped her foot on the floor to the rhythm of the music as she listened on her earbuds. The lead singer was belting out a ballad about regret and redemption. Even though most of the power was off in her office, there was enough illumination from the emergency ceiling light over her desk that she could still work and finish reviewing the lab reports on her desk, as she desperately wanted to go home and get some much-needed rest.

A hand gripped her by the shoulder. She jumped and spun around in her chair.

"You ass!" she said when she saw the big grin on Ron's face. She pulled out her earbuds and turned off the song.

"Hey, it's seven o'clock, shouldn't you be getting off?"

"What, with you?"

"That would be the general idea. You want to do it in the morgue?"

"Not likely. What are you doing here?"

"Dave and I just brought in another stiff."

"Who?"

"Danny Grimes. Talk about a mess."

"What happened?"

"Who knows? Dave's already gone, so if you're interested."

"You know what would happen if we got caught?"

"Adds to the excitement," Ron said still with the grin.

"How about we—?" Lucy stopped when she heard a loud noise outside in the corridor. "What was that?"

Ron stared at the door. "I don't know, big rats?" There were sounds of rending metal and heavy objects being thrown against the walls. He crossed the room and opened the door a crack. He peered into the gloomy hall. "I can't see a thing, it's too dark. You stay here, I'm going to have a look."

"Are you crazy? Don't go out there," Lucy pleaded.

"Lock the door after me," was all he said and slipped out into the hall.

Lucy rushed over and turned the lock. She gazed out the door window. The thick glass was reinforced with meshed wire in between the double panes for added security. The dim light inside her office refracted off the window making impossible to see anything in the hallway.

She heard Ron yell something and then scream. Heavy footfalls came down the hall. Ron's scream escalated into a high-pitched screech.

Suddenly, Ron's face was slammed into the window. His nose flattened as a giant hand gripped the back of his head and pressed him against the glass. Lucy could see the thick fingers and thumb digging into the sides of Ron's skull. Ron's eyes slowly bulged from the sockets. Blood wept from his tear ducts and out of his nostrils. His face contorted as he tried to speak but all that came out of his mouth were broken bits of teeth mixed with saliva and blood.

Lucy could hear a steady crunch.

And that's when Ron's head burst all over the glass.

***

The phone on Vera's desk rang. She looked down at the caller ID screen as she picked up the receiver. "It's Lucy. Poor girl must be working late again."

"Can I take that? I'd like to ask her something," Abel said.

"Sure," Vera said and handed the phone to the sheriff.

Abel put the receiver up to his ear but didn't say anything right away. "Lucy, calm down. This is Sheriff McGuire. I can't understand a word you're saying."

"What's wrong?" Kate asked.

Vera looked up with concern.

"Just stay where you are and keep your door locked," Abel instructed. "I'll be right there."

"Abel, what's happening?"

"Something just killed Ron Tully!"

24

Even though Abel told Kate to stay behind, she insisted on going along because as the doctor on duty, she was responsible for the medical staff of the hospital. They didn't hear anything coming down the rear stairwell except their own footsteps until they reached the bottom landing. There was so much noise and banging on the other side of the door that it sounded like junk caught up in a twister.

"What the hell is going on out there?" Kate said.

"I don't know but whatever it is, it's going berserk." Abel had drawn his revolver and was holding the gun in front of him. He peered through the small glass window. The corridor was tenebrous as the only overhead fluorescent light shining was down at the end of the hallway.

"What do you see?" Kate asked.

"Not much." As soon as he said that, an empty gurney flew down the hallway and careened off a wall. It flipped over and landed on its side. He cringed when he heard a deep roar and another crash.

"What in God's name was that?" Kate asked.

"Could be the creature from the convenient store."

"What's it doing here?"

"I have no idea." Abel listened for a moment but couldn't hear any more noise.

"Do you think it left?"

"Only one way to find out. Stay here while I go check."

"The hell. I'm coming too."

Abel slowly opened the door and stepped into the hall. The door leading outside was open and was hanging askew. He noticed that the Exit sign over the doorframe was not lit up.

"Dave or Ron must have forgotten to turn the power back on," Kate said.

"That's why the alarm didn't go off."

They took a couple steps and stopped. The door leading into the morgue was also damaged and dangled off its hinges.

"You don't think it could still be in there?" Kate asked.

Abel looked down at the floor and saw a trail of very large blood-smeared footprints coming from the morgue, down the hall, and leading outside through the rear doorway. "Judging by those tracks, I think it's gone."

He stepped into the room. Two gurneys were toppled over. Bud's naked and headless body was on the floor. The body bag containing Danny Grimes was still zipped up and lying a few feet away. A third gurney was still on its casters but was the most horrific.

"Oh my God!" Kate said. "Why would it do that?"

"Jesus."

The sheet had been ripped off of Ralph Tillerman's nude body. His ribcage was split apart and his abdomen cavity was a gaping hole. The man's heart and lungs were on the floor, along with coils of intestines and his other internal organs. His spine had been snapped clean in two and his waist and legs were separated six inches from his upper torso.

Kate stepped carefully around the room. She stood over the crudely autopsied remains then looked over at Abel. "Grab me that broom."

Abel retrieved the broom leaning against the wall and brought it over to Kate.

She held it bristles up and prodded the gory slop on the floor with the handle.

"What in the world are you doing?" Abel asked.

"This is weird. All of his organs are here but one."

"What's that?"

"His stomach. Do you see it anywhere?" Kate said and gazed about the floor.

Abel glanced around. "No, can't say I do."

Kate looked at Abel. "My God, we forgot about Lucy."

They rushed out of the morgue and made their way down the hall.

Ron was on the floor not too far from the door to the lab. His head looked like a gourd that had been backed over by a truck.

"Jesus," Abel said. He tried opening the door but it was locked so he knocked a couple times.

Lucy threw open the door and put her arms around him. "It killed Ron. I was so scared. Oh my God…" and then she burst into tears.

"It's okay, Lucy, we're here," Kate said and rubbed Lucy's back to console her.

Abel took a step back and let Kate take over as Lucy immediately went to the doctor for comfort. He heard footsteps and pointed his gun at a figure coming down the hall. "Who's there?"

"It's me. Grant. I came to visit Bess when Vera told me what happened."

"It's been one hell of a slaughter fest down here that's for sure." Abel's portable radio came on. "Sheriff McGuire," it was Gayle Becker at the answering service, dispatching a call. "There's been a complaint of shots being fired on Walnut Street."

Abel responded. "Thanks, Gayle but I have a bit of a situation here at the hospital."

"Just relaying the message, Sheriff. Have a nice evening." The radio clicked off.

"Don't the Levitt brothers live on Walnut?" Grant said.

"That's right," Abel said.

"Maybe you should go, make sure there's not more trouble," Kate said, her arm still around Lucy.

"What about this? This is a major crime scene."

"Don't worry," Kate said. "I'll seal off the ground floor and keep everyone out."

"All right."

"Mind if I tag along?" Grant said. "Bess is asleep and I didn't see any point in waking her. Besides, if it is the Levitts shooting up the town, you might need a little backup."

"Wouldn't mind the company."

25

The rain was coming down pretty hard by the time Abel and Grant arrived at the location where there had been shots fired.

Halsey, Rand, and Cobb Levitt were standing outside in the street, soaking wet and armed with rifles. Their monster truck was parked half on the sidewalk and half in the street.

Two of the truck's windows were smashed out.

Rand aimed at the big oak tree between the two houses across the street and fired off two shots.

"Damn fools," Abel said, getting out his side and drawing his revolver.

Grant climbed out, stood behind his opened door, and pointed his weapon over the top of the window frame.

"Put those rifles down before you kill someone!" Abel yelled, making sure he could be heard over the torrential downpour.

The Levitt brothers stood there like a trio of deaf mutes.

"Guns! Down now!"

Cobb was the first to put his gun on the ground. Rand stared at Abel for a few seconds then lowered his rifle and placed it by his feet.

"Back away," Grant said.

Rand and Cobb stepped back.

Halsey kept his rifle pointed at the oak tree.

"Not going to tell you again, Halsey!"

"I'm not giving up my gun, not with that thing out there!"

"What's out there?" Abel asked.

Halsey didn't reply at first then said, "Damn thing's on a rampage!"

The rear side window of the cruiser shattered.

Abel spun around and saw a gaping hole in the center of the safety glass. He immediately crouched and aimed his gun across the street.

"Abel, you okay?" Grant yelled from the other side of the car.

"Yeah."

"What was that? I didn't hear a shot."

71

Abel glanced over his shoulder and saw a grapefruit-size cobblestone on the shard-strewn back seat as the rain blew into the car.

"Someone threw a rock at us." He trained his gun on the oak tree, thinking whoever pitched the large stone was probably hiding there. He was surprised that the occupants of the two houses hadn't woken up and turned on some lights with all the commotion going on.

A pyramid-shaped pile of slick cobblestones was next to a driveway near an area that had been excavated for resurfacing—ammunition for their assailant.

Even though Abel was crouched behind the driver's door, he had parked parallel with the curb so he was vulnerable and exposed to another assault. He reached up and grabbed the spotlight handle, flicked the lamp on, and swiveled the beam on the oak tree, which cast a wide shadow between the brightly lit houses.

Halsey fired two shots at the tree.

"Damn it, Halsey," Abel cursed. "Put down that gun!"

Abel saw something fly out from behind the tree and as he turned, he saw a large rock stave in Cobb's face. The front of Cobb's head exploded like a watermelon. When the rock fell away, his forehead, cheekbones, and jawbone were caved in and looked like the inside of a gore-smeared bowl.

He teetered for a moment, and then, like a marionette whose puppeteer had just cut its strings, fell to the ground in a heap.

"Holy Christ," Rand yelled.

"Now do you believe me?" Halsey shouted.

"Abel, get back here with me. You're a sitting duck out there," Grant said.

Abel scooted onto the front seat and closed the door just as it took a direct hit.

The car rocked as though a cannonball had struck it.

Abel scampered out the passenger side and joined Grant. "Whatever it is, it sure has one hell'uva arm."

Halsey yelled, "Grover! Get your bony ass out here!"

The pit bull charged out the front door of Halsey's place, almost ripping the screen door off of its hinges. The dog growled menacingly and bolted down the steps, slipping and sliding on the wet concrete as it raced across the street.

"That's it!" Halsey cheered. "Flush the bastard out!"

Grover disappeared into the dark.

A loud roar boomed in the night.

Like a cranky lion at feeding time.

"What in blazes was that?" Abel said.

"I don't know," Grant replied.

Grover cried out with a pitiful yelp.

Abel and Grant gazed up like a couple of sports fans standing on the sideline, watching the football pass sail down the field, only instead of a pigskin, it was Grover that was flying across the street.

The dog landed on the sidewalk with a sickening splat.

"Damn thing killed my dog!" Halsey screamed with rage, readying his rifle.

Abel couldn't believe that the man's brother had just been killed and all Halsey was remorseful about was his dog. "Halsey, put that—"

Grant grabbed Abel by the arm. "I saw something!"

"What?"

"I'm not sure. But it was big. Went back toward the back alley."

Abel ducked inside the rain-drenched cruiser and scooted across the seat to get behind the wheel.

Before Grant could close his door, they were racing down the street to the first intersection. Abel hung a left, shot down a short block, and cut down the alleyway that stretched behind the houses.

"There! Up ahead!" Grant yelled, pointing out the windshield at the barely visible shape running ahead of them in the pouring down rain.

Abel glanced at the speedometer. "This is insane."

"I know. I can't see a thing."

"No, I mean we're almost doing thirty."

"Shit, look out!"

Abel slammed on the brakes. The car skidded to a stop.

The hulking giant stood in the rain and glared down at them through the windswept windshield. Abel had the wipers operating at full speed, but every time the blades cleared off the glass, the raindrops covered it back over.

Judging by what he could see, the creature had to be eight feet tall.

"Maybe you should call Animal Control," Grant said, nervously.

"You're the game warden."

The towering brute looked especially menacing as its leg blocked off the beam of the right headlamp and its form was silhouetted in the rain.

"The thing's huge!" Abel said, gawking at the broad shoulders and the over-developed upper torso that possessed enough super-human strength to shot-put a sixty-pound dog clear across a street.

"I'll say," Grant said, averting his eyes from the long phallic appendage hanging between its legs the split second the wiper blade passed over the windshield.

"Oh, shit," Abel said, when he spotted the large cobblestone in its right hand.

The beast slammed the rock down onto the hood of the car with such force that it punched a hole in the thick metal like it was a thin sheet of tin.

It reared back its arm and hurled the rock at the windshield.

"Get down!" Abel yelled.

They scrunched in their seats as the projectile struck the upper edge of the windshield and careened over the top, shattering the plastic emergency bar mounted on the roof into a thousand pieces.

Abel raised his head for a quick peek.

The beast was gone.

26

Abel pulled the hood of his poncho over his head as he got out of the car. He raced around to the back and popped the trunk. He grabbed one of the twelve-gauge Remington pumps from the cruiser's trunk, passed it to Grant, and handed him some cartridges.

"Did you see which way it went?" Grant asked, feeding a shell into the chamber.

"I'm thinking it went through there," Abel said, pointing the muzzle of his shotgun at the hole in a redwood fence big enough to drive a car through.

They ratcheted their guns in unison.

"Here, take this," Abel said. He handed Grant a flashlight and took one for himself.

"When's this rain ever going to let up?" Grant said.

"How smart do you think this thing is?"

"Smart enough to throw rocks with a high degree of accuracy. You do know if we're not careful, this thing will pound us into the ground like a couple of action heroes made out of Play-Doh."

"Thanks for the visual. Let's hope that doesn't happen. Come on. And stay close." Abel stepped through the opening in the fence and Grant followed as they entered the backyard.

It was coming down so hard that Abel had to squint to see where he was going.

He glanced down and saw a stepping-stone path that ran alongside a cottage behind the main house. "I know this place. Used to be a garage. Renters were growing weed inside, had more than forty wall sockets for their grow lights. It was a wonder the place didn't burn down."

He continued down the side of the cottage and stopped when he reached the front of the small structure. If he remembered right, the house was only twenty feet up ahead.

There was a loud crash followed by screeching metal and the cracking of timber.

"It's breaking down the door," Grant said, straining to see in the heavy rain.

Abel heard a strange sound like a saber swishing through the air.

"Get down!" he yelled and tackled Grant.

They were nearly decapitated when a wrought iron security screen door whizzed over their backs and smashed into the front of the cottage, shattering a plate-glass window and tearing out a section of aluminum siding.

"Threw that door like a damn Frisbee," Grant said.

They got up and strode warily across the lawn.

When they reached the rear of the house, they found the backdoor had been bashed in and was laying in the middle of the kitchen floor; the hinges ripped clean out of the splintered doorframe.

The kitchen looked like a demolition team had come in with sledgehammers and spent a few hours wrecking the place. Where in fact, it had been the raging beast that had ripped the cabinets off the walls and toppled the table, crushed the chairs underfoot before it yanked the refrigerator from the wall and pushed it over, spilling the contents all over the linoleum floor—and in less than thirty seconds. Abel stepped through broken glass and trampled food. He could feel the foundation tremble as the beast stormed through the house.

"Jesus, the thing's a damn wrecking ball," Grant said, following right behind Abel and wading through the mess.

Abel switched on his flashlight, as the rest of the home was pitch black. He shined the beam on the floor to make sure he wasn't going to trip or slide on anything that had fallen out of the fridge and almost stepped on a PSH take-home box.

The beast roared as it went berserk, slamming walls and toppling furniture.

"We have to stop this thing before it kills someone," Abel said.

A man and a woman screamed from a back bedroom.

"Shit!" Abel charged out of the kitchen and into the living room. Standing lamps were lying on the floor. A recliner was on its side. Knickknacks swiped off the bureau. The room looking like a twister had just passed through.

Abel shined his flashlight down the hallway.

The man kept yelling but was quickly silenced by what sounded like a pummeling blow, which made the woman scream even louder.

Then came a mighty roar and an explosion of shattering glass.

Abel and Grant charged down the hallway.

They halted at the bedroom door and shined their flashlights into the room.

The man on the mussed bed was on his stomach; his head turned facing the door.

"Isn't that Bernie Lambert?" Grant asked.

"Sure is. My God, it broke him in half," Abel said. Lambert's torso was under his bent legs, the soles of his bare feet resting on his shoulder blades. The man's spine had been completely crushed. He looked like a contortionist in red pajamas that had just been lifted out of a box.

Abel and Grant went into the room.

The sliding glass door had been shattered and shards of glass were strewn on the carpet and all over the cement patio outside.

They stepped over the bloody jagged pieces of glass sticking out of the sliding door's lower frame and went out onto the rain-drenched patio.

The sheriff and game warden followed the blood trail and found Bernie's wife in her nightdress lying facedown in the waterlogged grass, not too far from where they had entered through the hole in the fence.

By the looks of things, the beast had grabbed her by the ankle and dragged her outside.

Grant stood vigilant with his shotgun while Abel turned the woman over.

"Ah, jeez," Abel said. "I can't say for certain, but this is probably Cindy Lambert."

The woman's nightdress was ripped to shreds and stained with blood, the exposed flesh of her breasts and stomach deeply gouged. Her face was unrecognizable as her nose and skin were sliced off from being dragged over the sharp glass. Blood trickled out of a savage slit in her neck.

Somewhere in the rain, the beast roared victoriously.

27

Billy looked out the rear door of the steakhouse and saw the rain was still coming down but was more of a drizzle. The lull before the storm as the weatherman would always say. He pushed the door open with his shoulder and hefted two trash bags over to the dumpster.

He'd brought along the key to unlock the lid. He'd learned his lesson after having to clean up after the last scavenger. Luckily, Gordy hadn't been the wiser or Billy would have been seeking employment elsewhere.

A high volume of water was cascading off the roof into the gutters and coming out of the downspouts. Already puddles had started to form in the back parking lot.

He placed the two bags at the base of the dumpster and went to fish the key out of his pocket.

"Well, did you get it?" a rough voice said behind him.

Billy turned and saw Halsey and Rand Levitt standing in the light rain.

Halsey took a step toward him and gave him a stern look. "I won't ask you again."

"I have it," Billy replied reluctantly.

"Then hand it over."

Billy didn't move, debating if he should run back inside the building. He doubted if Halsey and Rand would come after him. Gordy didn't like it when people made trouble inside his restaurant.

One time, when an irate customer was giving Penny a hard time about his bill, Gordy came out from the kitchen and stood by the register. He never said a word. Just laid his meat cleaver on the counter in plain view. The customer quickly got the hint. He paid and—while being scrutinized by Gordy—handed a twenty-dollar bill to Penny for a tip and never came back.

Rand made the decision for Billy and blocked the rear door.

Halsey put his hand out palm up.

Billy knew there was no point in refusing the Levitts. The two of them would just pound the shit out of him and take the key he'd made that fit the lock to the backdoor to Tanner's hardware and hunting supply store.

"Promise me you won't hurt anyone."

"Billy, you know I can't do that."

Billy reached inside his trouser pocket and took out the key. He cocked his arm back like he was ready to throw it. "Promise!"

"You want me to bust him up?" Rand asked Halsey.

"Be my guest."

Rand pounded his fist into his palm. "This is going to be fun."

"All right, you win," Billy said and tossed the key to Halsey.

Halsey caught it.

"Just don't hurt them," Billy said.

"Oh, you mean like this," Rand said and slugged Billy in the stomach.

Billy grabbed his belly and dropped to his knees.

"And make sure you keep your mouth shut," Halsey warned.

Billy was too busy groaning to reply.

"Understand?" Rand said, cocking his fist back for another punch, but this time to the face.

"Yes…"

"Good. See that you do," Halsey said.

Billy watched the two men stride around the corner. He could hear doors opening and closing then the loud rumble of the monster truck's beefy engine. He wondered if Cobb had decided to remain in the truck as he wasn't as ruthless as Halsey and Rand and never wanted any part when it came to bullying Billy.

He never got a look at the truck as it sped away on the wet pavement, heading toward the main road on the other side of the restaurant.

Billy felt sick to his stomach, not from the punch but because of his betrayal to Kit and her grandfather. He'd just handed the key to the Tanner store to Halsey which meant that the Levitts could sneak in and steal anything they wanted whenever they wanted and not have to actually break into the place. They could take a little here, a little there, and old man Tanner wouldn't suspect a thing. He'd probably think he was getting senile or he had made an error in his inventory.

Each time the Levitts stole something, Billy would be further to blame.

There was no way he could let them get away with it. It was high time he stood up for himself. He slowly got to his feet and staggered in through the back door.

Penny had come from the dining area and was in the storeroom, grabbing a box of napkins. She saw Billy and called out, "You better get up front. There's a table needs clearing."

"I can't," Billy said taking off his apron.

"Why not?"

"I did something really stupid." Billy told Penny about sneaking Kit's key to her grandfather's store and making a copy for Halsey Levitt.

"Oh my God, Billy. Why would you even do that?"

"I can't get into it right now," he said, putting on his coat. "I have to go warn Mr. Tanner."

"Okay. I'll tell Gordy you had an emergency. There're only a few customers because of the storm so I guess I can handle it."

"Thanks, Penny."

"But you will be coming back, right?"

"Sure."

"Don't leave me hanging."

"I won't," Billy said as he dashed out through the back door.

28

Penny returned to the dining area and placed the box of napkins under the counter by the register. She grabbed a coffee pot and walked over to the tables.

Margery Simmons and Blanche Mayberry were seated across from each other at their favorite table, which was positioned against the wall under a large rectangular mirror framed in an elegant walnut with hand-carved wilderness animals.

Normally, the two women would only frequent the steakhouse once a month, being as that was all they could really afford, living off their dead husbands' pensions, but here they were again, only a day after Ralph Tillerman had dropped dead in the parking lot. Penny wondered if they were back to see if she would make a repeat performance and save another hapless diner from choking. She could imagine the two women sitting together on the couch watching NASCAR, hoping desperately for the racecars to crash.

"How are your meals?" Penny asked. Their coffee cups were still upside down, meaning they weren't ready for caffeine yet as they were sharing a large carafe of red house wine. The women had asked for a split order of the grilled bone steak as a twenty-ounce piece of meat was too much for either of them to eat on their own. Penny promised to adjust their bill accordingly.

"I sure would like to know what Gordy uses to marinate his meat," Blanche said grinning over at Margery.

"Blanche, behave," Margery replied and looked up at Penny to see if she was enjoying the joke.

"If you want, I could go ask him," Penny said.

"No, no, no," Blanche said with a sudden look of fright then giggled. "That's quite all right." She picked up her wineglass and polished it off. She poured herself another glass of wine from the decanter.

Penny gave them her standard smile and moved on to the next table. Hardin Lee was sitting by himself. The big truck driver was finishing up his meal. He sat back in his chair and pushed his plate to the middle of the table. He flipped his coffee cup over and held it up for Penny to fill.

"Got room for some dessert?" Penny asked, pouring the steaming coffee into his cup, already knowing the answer to her question. Hardin was always up for dessert and always ordered the French apple cobbler with two scoops of vanilla ice cream.

Hardin ignored the dessert menu tucked in the condiment holder and gave Penny a smile.

"I think I'll have the usual."

"Give me a sec and I'll get that for you."

"Take your time," Hardin said. He leaned his chair back against the wall on two legs under a large deer head with an enormous ten-point rack, mounted on the wall.

Penny thought she better check on Camden and Donna Rice seated by the window and see if there was anything she could get them before she prepared Hardin's dessert.

"You know, Penny," Camden said as she came over. "I put an extra fifty cents in that stupid newspaper box you have out front and it still wouldn't open."

"I'm sorry. Tell you what. Even though the restaurant really isn't responsible, I'll deduct it from your bill."

"That's so sweet," Donna said. "See, Camden. I told you she would reimburse us."

Penny heard a loud rumble outside followed by a bright blue flash on the windowpanes as a lightning strike lit up the night sky.

"Whoa!" Camden said, facing the window. "Did you see that?"

"That sure was a—" but then Penny stopped when the lights went out inside the restaurant. It was good that Penny had thought to light the candles on each table as they were the only source of illumination and flickered an ambient glow.

"Well, isn't this romantic," Donna said to her husband.

"Sure hope there's power when we get home."

"Penny!" Gordy called out from the kitchen. "Everything all right out there?"

"Yes, we're fine," Penny answered. Even though the grill and burners were gas and Gordy could still cook, she knew they would have to close the restaurant for the night as soon as everyone was through eating, as no other customers would be coming as long as the electricity was out.

Penny went behind the counter. She opened the clear plastic door on the cake and pie display and took out a pan of French apple cobbler. She cut out a generous-sized wedge and placed it on a plate. Leaning down, she opened the door to the small compact freezer tucked under the counter and grabbed a quart container of vanilla ice cream. She put two scoops on top of the plate of pie and returned the ice cream to the freezer.

Coming out from behind the counter, Penny started walking over to Hardin's table. She heard a loud crack outside and looked at a window just as the night lit up.

She caught a glimpse of the cars parked out front for a split second—and a giant figure standing on the walkway.

Penny closed her eyes and reopened them thinking she was just tired and she was seeing things.

The panes of glass in the front of the restaurant were mostly dark except for the reflecting glow of the candles on the tables. *What the heck did I just see?* she thought to herself.

"What's wrong, Penny? You act like you just saw a ghost," Hardin said, sitting forward in his chair.

"I thought I saw something outside," Penny said, still holding Hardin's dessert. She felt something drip along her hand and realized that she had been standing there long enough for the ice cream to start to melt. "Oh, gosh, I'm sorry." She went over and placed the plate in front of the big man.

"Thanks. Any chance on a refill," Hardin said and raised his empty cup.

"I'll be right back." Penny was heading over to grab the coffee pot when she heard a loud explosion of shattering glass. The newspaper box flew into the dining room and slammed into Camden, flipping him right out of his chair.

Donna's eyes grew wide with fright.

Blanche and Margery screamed.

Penny looked down at the floor. The damaged newspaper box was on top of Camden's head and chest. The door had sprung open and the latest editions of the *Porterville Gazette* had fallen out, along with some spilled coins.

Blood slowly pooled out from under the newspaper box and seeped into the carpet.

"What…just…?" Donna tried to say, but was still in shock.

Penny glanced up.

A giant hairy arm reached in, grabbed Donna by the hair, and yanked her out through the busted-out window.

"Jesus Christ, what the hell was that?" Hardin said, jumping up from his table.

"I don't know," Penny said. "It happened so fast."

Blanche and Margery were still screaming, only louder.

"Will you two *shut* the hell up!" Hardin yelled.

The two hysterical women gaped at the big man and quieted down but kept sobbing.

"Gordy!" Hardin hollered. "You got a gun back there?"

Penny looked over at the pass-thru window and saw Gordy's face. "What's going on out there?" he yelled.

"Something just broke—" Penny started to say but stopped when the front door smashed open.

She turned and saw the beast. It stood over eight feet tall and was covered with thick matted hair. It looked especially sinister in the gloom, as most of the candles had blown out when the big pane of glass was smashed. Sheets of rain were blowing in.

The massive creature took a step forward.

Penny swore the foundation shook.

Hardin grabbed his steak knife off the table. "Penny, you and the women, get in the back." He kicked his chair out of the way ready to fight. Even though he was a big man at six-foot-two and weighed a good two hundred fifty pounds, he looked puny matched up against his taller, six-hundred-pound adversary.

The beast sensed the threat and roared. It glared at Hardin and charged across the room. Everything on the tabletops shook as the giant creature stomped over, grabbed Hardin, and hoisted him in the air.

"Son of a bitch," Hardin yelled and stabbed the monster in the shoulder with his steak knife.

The beast yowled and impaled Hardin on the deer antlers on the wall.

Hardin hung there, blood-red horn tips protruding out of his chest, his boots dangling two feet off the floor. Black blood gushed out of his mouth as his eyes rolled back.

Blanche and Margery began screaming again.

The beast turned and faced the women. It saw its reflection in the large mirror above their table and snarled, thinking it was seeing another menacing creature.

The two women cowered in their chairs as the beast smashed its fist into the mirror. Large shards of glass rained down on Blanche and Margery, slicing their heads and hands. The beast grabbed a corner of the heavy frame, ripped the mirror from the wall, and sent it crashing down on top of the women, killing them instantly.

Penny backed around the counter, trying not to make any noise.

The beast turned and glared at her.

She bolted down the length of the counter and dashed through the swinging door that led to the kitchen.

The beast stormed after her, tossing chairs and tables out of its way.

"Gordy!" she yelled.

She saw her boss standing by the walk-in freezer. She glanced over her shoulder and saw the beast plow into the kitchen.

Gordy pulled open the heavy door.

Penny could feel the hot breath of the beast on the back of her neck.

Gordy stepped inside the freezer and was about to close the door when Penny dove in and her boss closed the door.

It was pitch dark until Gordy turned on a flashlight.

"For a second there, I thought…" Penny was saying then stopped when she saw the strange look in Gordy's eyes, confirming what she had been thinking. If she hadn't slipped through the door when she did, he would have left her outside to die.

The thick door shook as the beast pounded on the metal. Penny faced the door, fearing it would punch its way through.

She glanced over at Gordy. He looked concerned but not surprised that the beast was outside battering the door.

"What is that thing?" Penny asked, but Gordy ignored her like she wasn't even there.

"Fine," she said and sat down on a blue ice chest with wheels, parked against the wall next to an identical cooler.

Gordy turned when he realized what she was sitting on. His eyes narrowed and he gave her a menacing look.

Goose pimples ran up and down her arms.

She didn't know what scared her the most: being trapped inside the walk-in freezer with her creepy boss or the beast outside hammering on the door.

29

Lottie Brand hated her job. Sure, she didn't have a boss breathing down her neck telling her what to do and constantly correcting her if she made a mistake, but it was boring working alone with no one to talk to. Tonight was especially dull as the storm was keeping customers away. She debated if she should close up early but knew if she did, she would probably get reamed for doing so.

She hadn't had a customer in the last two hours and spent her idle time rearranging the different packets of coffee blends and making sure the brewing machine and the espresso maker were ready if a customer should happen to drive up. She had her portable radio for company tuned to her favorite hip hop station, but the reception had been poor and filled with static at times from all the lightning she had been seeing out the drive-up window.

The rain would come down hard for a time then let up just to resume into a deluge. She could see a storm drain that had gotten clogged and water was beginning to back up into the parking lot. She almost wanted to cover her ears as the rain pounded on the metal kiosk roof. It was enough to drive her mad. Maybe it was time to pack it up and call it a night. She didn't like the idea of driving home in this weather though it was only five miles away but she didn't see any point in staying either as it was only going to get worst. For all she knew, the road to her apartment was washed away.

It would take her twenty minutes to empty the machines and clean them for the next day. Then she could bundle up, get in her car, and drive home. She'd parked her AMC Gremlin subcompact by the exit door so she wouldn't get too wet when she left.

The stupid ceiling fan had gone out an hour ago so she was forced to open the sliding glass door of the drive-up window a crack to get some fresh air.

Lottie turned and held a pitcher under a spout, draining the hot water out of the reservoir on the espresso machine to dump down the drain.

Her little radio played a Madonna song but as Lottie started to sing along, a lightning bolt lit up the inside of the kiosk and she saw a huge shadow superimposed over her and the wall she was facing.

She heard the glass door on the pass-thru grind open and then a terrible smell wafted into the small structure. It was like the rankest garbage she had ever smelled had just been tossed in through the window.

Lottie slowly turned. Her eyes widened with fear.

A gorilla-sized hand reached in to grab her. Lottie jumped back and the hot water in the pitcher splashed up into her face. She screamed and flailed about, blinded by the scalding liquid. She searched and found the doorknob to the exit door. She pushed the door open and stumbled out into the rain.

The beast snatched her up with its powerful arms and held her in a bone-crushing bear hug; her face pressed flat against its wet fur, the malodorous stench taking her breath away. She could hear and feel its heart thumping loudly in its chest.

One sudden compression and Lottie was dead.

30

Wiley Tanner stood at the front window of his store, looking out at the nearly empty parking lot as the rain pelted the glass. "Guess we might as well close up early," he said and turned to Kit who was leaning on the display case of fishing reels.

"Are you sure?" Kit asked. "I don't mind staying a little longer. You never know, someone might come in for some foul weather gear."

"If they don't have it by now, I doubt some fool's going to come out in this soaker and get drenched buying a rain slicker."

"I'll start turning off the lights."

"That's okay, I'll do that. You know what, I don't feel much like cooking. You wouldn't mind going over to the deli at the supermarket and have Vern make me up one of those Dagwood sandwiches. Maybe have him throw in a pint or two of that potato salad of his."

"Sure thing, Grandpa."

Wiley pulled out his billfold, plucked out a twenty-dollar bill, and handed it to Kit.

"I won't be long," she said and grabbed her coat.

The wind was blowing like crazy when she stepped outside. She zipped up her coat and pulled her hood over her head. If she didn't know any better, she would have sworn it was hailing. The heavy raindrops felt like she was being targeted by a bunch of kids with pellet guns.

She glanced across the parking lot and saw the outside neon and interior lights were all on at the Coffee Mill drive-thru kiosk. *Really, Lottie, you think people are going to come out in this storm just so they can have one of your fancy lattes?* Was she out of her mind?

Kit looked over at the front entrance to the supermarket and saw Tim Eddleman pushing an empty shopping cart that he had retrieved from the parking lot. His hair was sopping wet and he looked soaked to the bone despite wearing a rain jacket.

Kit could feel the electricity in the air as a thunderclap boomed followed by a white zigzag of lightning.

"Hey, Kit," Tim called out.

"Hey yourself," Kit replied as the automatic doors opened and she stepped inside the supermarket. It wasn't a very big store. There were six aisles of canned and dried goods, a small bakery, a produce area, the refrigerated beverages and frozen foods, and the butcher's section with a delicatessen.

As Kit passed through, she waved to Cassidy who was at the checkout stand ringing up Susie Milcher who had her nose in a tabloid magazine she had taken off the rack as she took one item at a time out of her full shopping cart and placed it on the conveyor belt. Kit could tell Cassidy was becoming a little perturbed as she impatiently waited to scan the merchandise slowly trickling her way. Luckily, there were no other customers waiting in line after Suzie.

Roger Clemens was standing in the cereal aisle and was gazing at the large selection, deciding which brand to put in his handbasket.

"Evening, Mr. Clemens," Kit said.

The tall man looked her way. "Oh, hi there, Kit." He had a perplexed look on his face.

"Anything wrong?" she asked.

"Dr. Wilson says I should lay off the bacon and eggs and eat more cereal as my cholesterol is high. Got any suggestions?"

"Sure." Kit looked at the shelf and pulled down a box of organic cereal. She glanced at the back of the box. "I eat this myself. Cinnamon oat clusters. It's gluten-free and is an excellent source of fiber. You can eat it with almond milk or right out of the box, whichever you prefer." She handed the box to Mr. Clemens.

He smiled and said, "Well, you sold me. Thanks, Kit."

"Anytime. Glad I could help."

The man smiled and sauntered over to the produce section.

She continued on down the aisle until she came to the long glass display case in front of the butcher's station with the cutting blocks and meat slicing machines on the other side. A third of the case was reserved for various types of fresh fish on ice such as brook trout, crappie, bluegill, catfish, and small tubs of crayfish. Rump roasts, steaks, chops, and plastic trays of sausage and hamburger straight from the meat grinder made up the other two-thirds.

The butcher, Vern Thompson, had removed the circular blade from one of the meat slicing machines and was wiping it down before putting it back on. He looked up when Kit hit the small domed bell on the top of the display case.

"What can I get you, Kit?" Vern put the blade down, came over, and rested his big hands on the counter.

"My grandfather sent me over. He'd like a big triple-decker and a quart of potato salad."

"Coming right up."

"Is Macy around?"

"I think she's in the break room."

"I'm going to pop in and say hi. Won't be long."

"I'll have your order ready when you come back," Vern said, and turned to compile the makings for Wiley's sandwich.

Kit walked over to a set of two large rubber doors and pushed through into the warehouse part of the supermarket. There were rows of shrink-wrapped merchandise on pallets stacked six feet high that would later be broken down to restock the shelves in the store.

She found Macy in the break room, sitting at a table surrounded by five other vacant plastic chairs. Two vending machines were against a wall: one with soda beverages and bottled waters, the other with bags of snack chips and candy.

An open take-home box with the emblem PSH on the lid was sitting in front of Macy. She held a fork and knife in her hands and was slicing tiny slivers of steak and popping them in her mouth. She looked up guiltily when Kit entered.

Macy chewed fast and swallowed. "Uh, hi, Kit."

"It's okay, don't mind me."

"I can't help it. It's so good," Macy said, wiping her chin then closing the lid on the take-home box.

"Don't let me ruin your break."

"Just spare me the lectures on the evils of eating meat."

"Look what happened to your boss."

"Yeah, that was really weird."

"Think you might get his job?"

"Kit! How can you say something like that? He's only been dead a day."

"Well, do you?"

Macy gave Kit a sheepish grin. "I sure the hell hope so."

"You're bad."

"I know. You still seeing Billy Boggs?"

"On and off," Kit said. "I don't know what to do."

"Why do you waste your time with that loser?"

"Now you're starting to sound like my mom."

"How *is* she by the way?"

"She's doing okay."

Macy started to get up from the table when she froze. "Kit, did you hear that?"

"Hear what?"

"I thought I heard a scream."

Kit listened for a moment and then she heard it too. "Sounds like someone from inside the store."

Macy left her take-home box on the table and ran after Kit as they raced out of the break room and pushed through the big rubber doors into the store.

"Who screamed?" Macy asked Vern, standing behind the meat display.

"Who else? Suzie Milcher," Vern answered back, shaking his head.

"Is she all right?" Kit asked.

"She's done this before. She'll scream and claim she saw a rat running around the store. Threaten to tell everyone if we don't give her a discount on her groceries."

"Macy, that's extortion. You need to tell the sheriff."

"Ralph always thought it was simpler to just knock fifty percent off her grocery bill and give her something for free like a big watermelon than take the chance of her fabricating stories and spreading them all around town."

"Well, Ralph's not here, now is he?" Kit said, and then dreaded her words for sounding callous.

Suzie screamed again.

"I better shut her up before she scares off the rest of the customers," Macy said.

Kit and Macy strode up the aisle toward the checkout stand. Cassidy was huddled on the floor by the register while Suzie Milcher stood next to the magazine rack screaming her fool head off.

"What in the world are you screaming about? Don't tell me you saw a mouse," Macy said, walking toward the hysterical woman.

Suzie pointed to the automatic front doors.

Kit turned and saw Tim Eddleman backing into the store. He was holding onto the handle of a shopping cart and keeping it between him and a giant monstrous creature that looked like a huge grizzly bear standing on its hind legs. The beast reached down and grabbed the front of the shopping cart and lifted it in the air. Tim was reluctant to let go, and was hoisted off his feet.

The beast grabbed Tim by the neck, slammed the shopping cart on the floor, and stuffed the bag boy inside the wire carrier. When Tim's arms and legs dangled out, the creature roughly shoved them in.

Kit could hear Tim's bones snapping as he hollered in pain.

The beast silenced him with a pile-driving blow to the head.

"Cassidy, get back here!" Macy yelled, but the grocery clerk was too frightened to move.

Roger Clemmens was standing at the end of the cereal aisle. He took one look at the towering beast and dropped his basket.

Kit glanced out the through the front windows when she heard an explosion and saw a lightning bolt striking a transformer on a power pole outside. Sparks flew everywhere as the casing blew apart and scattered all over the parking lot.

The beast looked over its shoulder when it heard the loud noise. Thinking that it might be in danger, it grabbed the shopping cart with Tim stuffed inside and propelled it on its wheels toward the front of the store. The automatic doors began to open but then the power went out and the lights shut off. The shopping cart got halfway through the entranceway before wedging between the doors.

Macy started to back away toward the rear of the store. The emergency generator turned on but only a few of the overhead lights came back on.

Kit looked over at Cassidy who was still cowering behind the checkout stand. "Cass, get up. It's not safe here."

Suzie stopped screaming and fainted dead away, careening into the magazine rack and taking it down with her as she fell.

The beast stomped over to the checkout stand. It looked down at the petrified woman sitting on the floor with her arms wrapped around her knees. Cassidy lowered her head, too afraid to look up. The giant creature let out a deep-throated huff then turned and started lumbering down the aisle toward the back of the store.

Kit saw Roger Clemmens duck behind a stand of apples and oranges in the produce section. She glanced over at Vern as she ran by. "There's a wild animal loose in the store. It just killed Tim," she yelled.

"What?" Vern said. He picked up a meat cleaver and came out from behind the counter. He stormed up the aisle but when he saw the beast coming at him, he froze in his tracks. "What in God's name?"

He held up the cleaver to show he meant business.

"I don't know if that's a good idea," Kit said.

The beast glared at the butcher.

"Get in the back and call the sheriff," Vern shouted and ran at the giant creature, swinging his meat cleaver.

The beast stepped out of the path of the sharp blade and grabbed Vern's arm as it passed by. The next thing Kit heard—besides Vern's bellowing cry—was the sickening sound like a turkey leg being wrenched off the bird.

Kit fled through the big rubber doors. She found Macy in the break room, rummaging through one of the lockers used by the employees.

Macy looked up when Kit bolted in. "I can't find my phone. I thought it was in my purse but it's not. I must have left it in the manager's office."

Kit heard heavy footsteps outside and turned.

The beast had followed her into the warehouse. It stood in the doorway and had to lower its head in order to fit through. It looked at the take-home container on the table then glowered at Macy. The creature stomped over and snatched Macy up. It flung her across the room like a rag doll into the snack food vending machine, smashing the glass.

Macy fell back onto the floor. The beast came over, grabbed the top of the vending machine, and toppled it on top of the assistant manager—never to become store supervisor—lying amid the crushed chip bags.

Kit moved to the corner of the room. There was no way for her to escape. She looked up and saw the beast staring down at her with its black orbs. It was breathing heavy, snorting like a lathered horse after a long hard run.

She could feel her heart pounding in her chest, ready to explode.

Kit closed her eyes and prayed her death would be quick and merciful.

31

"What took you so long?" Abel asked when Dave Rockford finally showed up with the hospital van and parked behind the police cruiser in the back alley.

"Sorry, Sheriff. Had a time finding the keys," Dave apologized as he climbed out into the pouring rain.

"Where'd you find them?"

"They were in Ron's pocket."

"Oh. Sorry you had to deal with that."

"That's okay. What do we have?"

"Bernie Lambert and his wife, Cindy."

"Man, people are dropping like flies in this town," Dave said. He went around to the back of the van, opened the doors, and pulled out the collapsible gurney. He looked through the hole in the fence where a few of the boards were missing. "I'm going to need some help."

"Sure," Abel said. "Go ahead and get Cindy ready. Grant and I'll carry the gurney through."

Dave grabbed two folded body bags and stepped through the opening in the fence while Abel and Grant broke the gurney down to a stretcher and carried into the backyard.

"What the heck happened here?" Dave asked as he laid out one of the body bags next to Cindy Lambert's body and pulled down the zipper.

"Something broke into their house and attacked them."

"Sure did a number on her."

"Wait till you see Bernie," Grant said.

Dave grabbed the woman by the shoulders while Abel helped with the feet and they placed her inside the body bag. They carried the corpse to the van and lifted the body bag onto another gurney already inside the back of the vehicle.

"Where's the other body?" Dave asked as they returned to the backyard.

"Through there," Abel pointed. "Careful of the glass."

The three men entered the bedroom through the gaping hole in the sliding glass door. Abel shined his flashlight on Bernie Lambert's misshaped body that looked like an end table.

"How am I going to fit him in a body bag looking like that?" Dave asked.

"Maybe we can straighten him out," Grant said.

"Jesus, what a night." Abel went over to one side of the bed while Grant stood on the other. They each grabbed one of Bernie's ankles and lifted them back, straightening out his legs.

"It's almost like his upper torso and legs aren't even connected," Grant said.

"The thing must have pulverized his spine."

Dave placed the body bag on the bed and they rolled Bernie Lambert inside.

After they had carried the corpse out to the van, Dave shut the double doors. "I guess I'll see you back at the morgue."

"Not so fast," Abel said. "There's one more stop."

"You mean there's more?"

"Cobb Levitt."

"If this keeps up, we're going to run out of room at the morgue." Dave got in the hospital van and followed Abel and Grant in the cruiser. When they arrived at the Levitt's house, the monster truck was gone.

Abel got out of the Crown Victoria and looked around. Grant opened his door and climbed out. Dave pulled up at the curb and opened his window. "Where's the body?"

"I don't know. It was right here," Abel replied staring down at the rain-swept street.

Grant walked over to the sidewalk. "Their dog is gone as well."

Abel looked over at the Levitt house but there were no lights on. "Halsey and Rand must have taken Cobb and Grover."

"But where to?" Grant asked.

"I have no idea."

32

The Porterville Hardware and Hunting Supply went dark. Wiley approached the window and saw sparks shooting off the top of a power pole in the parking lot. The lights were dim at the supermarket and out at the Coffee Mill kiosk. He strained his eyes but couldn't see much and figured the whole town was blacked out.

Wiley shuffled to the camping supplies. He groped around in the gloom and found a battery-operated lantern that was on display. He turned the switch, illuminating a small portion of the store.

He hoped Kit was okay. The loud thunder reverberated through the walls like the sound was originating inside the store.

Wiley heard a bang in the back storeroom. He knew it couldn't be Kit because she would come back through the front entrance not the back door. He held the lantern up and traipsed to the door leading to the storage area. When he opened the door, two dark figures were just coming in through the back door.

"Who's there?" Wiley snarled.

"Hell, Halsey, I thought you said the store was closed," Rand Levitt said.

"There weren't any lights. How'd I know he'd still be here," Halsey answered.

"You're those damn Levitt brothers! Where the hell is the other one?"

"Never you mind. Shut your mouth and go sit over there on that crate."

"The hell I will," Wiley snapped. "Get out of my store. How'd the hell you get in anyway? Door was locked."

Halsey held up his hand. "You might say we got ourselves a key to the kingdom."

"How'd you get that?"

"Shut up old man and do what my brother told you," Rand said and pushed Wiley over to the crate. When the storeowner refused to sit, Rand smacked him on the side of the head and the old man fell back, landing hard on the wooden box. "Stay put or I'll clobber you again. And keep your mouth shut." Rand found some rope and tied Wiley's hands behind his back and bound his ankles together so he couldn't get up and walk.

Wiley sat helpless and watched as the two men began filling duffle bags with expensive hunting supplies. Halsey went into the store and a moment later, there was a loud crash of breaking glass. He came back carrying an armful of rifles. "Grab some handguns out of the display. And get as much ammunition as you can."

Rand hurried into the store, carrying a couple of empty expandable duffels by their handles.

Five minutes later, he was back lugging the heavy bags. He walked by Wiley and went out the opened back door and hoisted the bags into the back of the big truck.

"What do you think, we got enough?" Rand asked Halsey when he came back inside.

"Yeah, I think we made a good haul," Halsey said, wadding up the money he had stolen from the register and putting it in his shirt pocket.

"What do we do about him?" Rand asked.

"You know old man, you weren't supposed to be here," Halsey said.

"Where'd you expect me to be? It's my damn store."

"Not for long."

"What do you mean?"

"You think we're going to just leave you here, so you can tell the sheriff?"

"That's exactly what I'm going to do!"

"No, I think you're going to have a little accident. Lights go out, an old guy like you can get pretty clumsy, knocking stuff over. Might even burn the place down."

"Now, you wait a minute."

"Rand, go get some lighter fluid."

Halsey's brother wasn't gone for more than fifteen seconds when he was back with a large plastic bottle of charcoal lighter fluid. He began spraying the flammable liquid over anything that looked highly combustible.

"You know, you don't have to do this."

"By the time the fire truck arrives, we'll be long gone," Halsey said, as Rand squeezed the last drop out of his container and threw it on the floor.

Rand had also found a box of long stick matches. He began taking them out one by one and striking them on the side of the carton and tossing them on the floor. The lighter fluid quickly ignited into small fires.

"Be seeing you in the hereafter," Halsey said with a laugh as he and Rand headed out the back door.

"You better pray you don't, you bastard," Wiley cursed as the storage area began to fill with smoke. He tried to get loose but the knots were too snug. He counted five separate fires. Even though they seemed to be getting bigger the flames hadn't spread—not yet. He wondered what was keeping Kit and why she hadn't returned. He wasn't ready to die just yet, certainly not by the hand of those lowdown Levitt brothers. If it was the last thing he did, he swore he would...

Someone came through the back door.

"What, you forgot something?" Wiley yelled, expecting it to be either Halsey or Rand.

"It's me, Mr. Tanner. Billy Boggs."

"My lord. Billy, cut me loose."

"I will, but you have to hold on."

"Can't you see the place is on fire?"

Billy ran across the room and grabbed a fire extinguisher off the wall. He came running back and began spraying white frothy foam over the flames. He went from one fire to the next, laying down the fire retardant. When the canister went dry, he bolted into the store and came back with another fire extinguisher and put out the other fires.

Satisfied that he had smothered the flames, Billy came over, took out his buck knife, and freed Wiley.

"Thanks, Billy. If you hadn't showed up when you did, I'd have been one toasty marshmallow."

"I'm sorry, Mr. Tanner."

"For what, Billy? You saved my life."

"But it's my fault they did this. I saw them leave. I had no idea this would happen. You have to believe me," Billy said, almost in tears.

"What are you talking about?"

"I stole Kit's key for the back door of the store and made a copy for Halsey Levitt."

"Why in tarnation would you do that?"

"Because if I didn't, he said he would hurt Kit."

"I'm going to shoot the bastard."

"I came here to tell you what I had done but I got here too late."

"No, son. You got here just in the nick of time."

"Where is Kit? I need to apologize to her. Do you think she'll forgive me?" Billy asked.

"Well, you'll have to ask her yourself. She went over to the supermarket to pick up some food for me but she hasn't come back yet. To tell you the truth, I'm getting a little concerned."

"Don't worry, Mr. Tanner. I'll find her," Billy said and ran out the door.

33

Billy made double sure that the Levitt brothers were gone and hadn't decided to come back then dashed over to his Honda parked behind the dumpster. He opened the door and got behind the wheel. It took him three tries before the stubborn engine started.

He went down the alley and turned up the narrow thoroughfare separating the supermarket and the hardware store that delivery trucks used to access the rear loading docks.

Instead of driving into a parking stall, Billy pulled up at the curb in front of the supermarket. He jumped out of the car and walked around the front bumper.

Someone had left a shopping cart packed with stuff stuck between the automatic doors. It was mostly dark inside the store with the exception of a few glowing emergency lights.

The rain was coming down in buckets, so Billy hurried under the overhang by the entrance. That's when he actually saw what was jammed inside the shopping cart.

"Oh my God," he yelled, unable to comprehend what had happened to Tim Eddleman who looked like a human pretzel.

The only way into the store was to climb over the mangled bag boy. Billy tried not to look directly into Tim's mashed face. He leaned forward, grabbed the edges of the automatic doors and managed to pull himself up and over the cart. He jumped down on the floor.

He heard something bump near the checkout stand.

"Who's there?"

Billy took a couple wary steps and tried to see over the conveyor belt. He saw the crown of someone's head and came closer. "Cassidy, is that you?" He went over and knelt beside the grocery clerk to see if she was hurt or needed help. She gazed up at Billy with a vacant look in her eyes.

"What happened?" Billy asked.

"It was a...monster."

"Monster? What are you talking about?" Billy glanced over and saw Suzie Milcher sprawled under the magazine rack. Her eyes were wide open staring up at the ceiling and it was obvious by the blank look on her face she was dead.

Billy grabbed Cassidy by the shoulders and shook her. "Cassidy, where's Kit?"

At first, Cassidy didn't respond, so Billy gave her another shake.

"In the back."

"Okay, stay right here," he said but felt stupid for saying that as he knew it would probably take a stick of dynamite to get her out from under the checkout stand.

He headed down the canned vegetable aisle and when he reached the produce area, Roger Clemmens popped his head up and whispered. "Billy, over here."

"Mr. Clemmens, what's going on?" Billy asked, darting over to the stand of peaches, apples, and nectarines.

"Keep your voice down."

As soon as Billy was close enough, Mr. Clemmens reached up and pulled him down onto the floor.

Billy was about to object when Mr. Clemmens nodded his head in the direction of the produce display against the wall with misters keeping the greens fresh.

A giant creature was standing there. It grabbed a head of lettuce and consumed it in two bites. From the back, it looked like a brawny bear or maybe a hairy ape. It was well over eight feet tall and had hands the size of catcher's mitts.

"We should make a run for it," Mr. Clemmens said.

"I can't leave until I find Kit."

"Kit's dead."

"No."

"I saw it go in the back of the store after her and Macy. They never came out."

"I can't leave until I'm sure."

"Suit yourself. I'm going." Mr. Clemmens was too busy watching the massive animal and wasn't looking where he was going. He bumped into the piled fruit and sent the whole lot cascading onto the floor.

The beast spun around and glared at Mr. Clemmens.

Mr. Clemmens turned in a panic and slipped on the fruit scattered all over the floor. He started scrambling on his hands and knees. Billy kept his head down and moved around the stand, hoping the creature didn't see him.

He watched in horror as Mr. Clemmens screamed and was picked up off the floor.

Billy knew there was nothing he could do to help the man. If he tried to intervene, he would only share the same fate; so he moved silently away and headed toward the back of the store.

He was almost to the meat department when his foot struck something metallic on the floor. He cringed as it skidded across the tile and banged up against a steel rack.

It was a bloodied meat cleaver.

Various fish and slabs of meat were strewn all over the floor.

Billy turned and looked inside the display case where the clear plastic cover had been smashed out and saw Vern Thompson's severed head on the pink-colored ice.

"Holy shit!" Billy yelled. He turned and looked back afraid that he had just given his position away, but Mr. Clemmens was screaming so loud he doubted if the beast had heard him.

Billy dashed over to the big rubber doors and pushed his way through. He stepped into the warehouse and saw the door leading into the break room. He went inside. The first thing he saw was someone's arm sticking out from under a vending machine that had been flipped over onto the floor.

"Jesus, Kit!" Billy ran over, grabbed the lip of the machine and tried to lift it but it was way too heavy. "Oh my God, no."

"Billy," a voice whispered.

"What?" Billy looked around the gloomy room. He saw a dark mass huddled in the corner. "Kit?" He rushed over and put his arms around her. "Mr. Clemmens said you were dead."

"I thought I was too."

"What happened in here?" Billy looked over at the toppled vending machine. "Is that Macy?"

"Yes. Billy, it was so strange. When that thing came in here, it became so angry when it saw Macy, it killed her. It could have killed me too but for some reason, it didn't?"

"Can we get out through the back?"

"I don't think so. The rollup door is probably locked."

"Any idea where the key would be?"

"Macy should have one."

"Well, we can forget that. That vending machine weighs a ton. We're going to have to go out the front way. Ready?"

"Yeah, but is that thing still inside the store?"

"What do you think?" Billy said and cocked his head toward the doorway.

Mr. Clemmens's screams could be heard echoing in the store.

"As soon as we step foot inside the store, *run!*"

Billy held Kit's hand and they left the break room. When they reached the big rubber doors, Billy stuck his head out. He could hear the creature snarling and thrashing about on the other side of the aisle.

"Come on, let's go!" Billy ran toward the front of the store, Kit right at his side.

When he looked over his shoulder, he saw the mammoth creature. It looked grotesque with so much blood covering its face and chest. It flung something on the floor that made a wet splat then chased after them.

Billy didn't even bother to get Cassidy's attention as she would have only gotten them killed, refusing to leave her hidey-hole. He pulled Kit along and shoved her in front of him as they dashed toward the narrow opening between the automatic doors.

"Up and over as fast as you can," Billy said.

Billy gave Kit a boost as she jumped up onto the top of the shopping cart. Her foot came down on Tim Eddlemen's mutilated body and she almost fell, but then she regained her balance and leaped out of the store. Billy was right behind.

"Get in my car." Billy ran around the Honda, yanked open the driver's door, and jumped in. He fumbled with the key and glanced over wondering why Kit hadn't gotten into the car.

She banged on the window. "Billy, open the door, it's locked!"

Billy stretched across the seat and lifted the door lock knob.

The six-hundred-pound creature ran full bore into the sliding door and shattered the glass as it smashed through.

Billy inserted the key, turned the ignition, but the engine only stuttered.

Kit yanked her door open and jumped in.

Billy tried again with no luck.

The beast charged and slammed into the side of the small compact car, almost rocking it over.

Billy cranked the key and the engine came to life. He stomped on the gas pedal and the Honda screeched through the parking lot. He looked in the rearview mirror and saw the creature lope away into the night.

34

"Are you okay?" Billy asked as he drove back around the rear of the supermarket and headed down the service alley.

"I'm a little shaken. Is there anyone back at the market? I mean alive."

"Cassidy's probably the only one."

"Shouldn't we go back for her?" Kit asked.

"She won't come with us. I tried." Billy pulled up behind the hardware store. He got out of the car and waited for Kit at the rear door, which was propped open with a cardboard box.

"Billy, I smell smoke."

"The Levitt brothers tried to burn the place down."

"What?"

"Don't worry, I put the fire out."

"You did? Why were you here?"

"I was looking for you."

"But why?"

"I'll tell you later. We better go inside."

"Oh my God. Is my grandfather all right?"

"Yeah, he's fine."

They entered the gloomy storage room. The smell of smoke was stronger inside the building and there was ash floating in the air.

Wiley was sitting in a canvas chair when they came into the store. He had a double-barrel shotgun resting across his knees. His face brightened when he saw Kit but then frowned when he saw that she was empty-handed. "Hey, where's my grub?"

"Sorry, Grandpa, but there's been some trouble," Kit said.

"You're telling me. Take a look at my store. Damn hooligan Levitts."

"You don't understand. People were killed in the supermarket."

"By who?"

"Not who, what," Billy said. "It's some giant beast. We almost didn't get away."

"It killed Macy Givens," Kit said.

"And Mr. Clemmens and Suzie Milcher," Billy added. "The butcher too."

"Vern?" Wiley said. "Damn, I was really looking forward to that sandwich."

"We need to go see if my mom is okay," Kit said.

"At the hospital? Let's go," Wiley said and slowly got to his feet. "But I'm bringing this along." He waved the shotgun. "What was this thing again?"

"I don't know. All I can tell you its big and mean," Kit replied.

"Come on, I'll drive," Billy said.

"Maybe we should take my grandfather's car, seeing as you've been having trouble starting yours."

"Sure, why not," Billy said. "Wouldn't want to get stranded in a night like this, especially with that creature out there."

Wiley fished in his trouser pocket and threw Billy the keys. "You go ahead and drive, son."

They went outside in the pouring rain and rushed over to an old-model four-door Jeep with veneer paneling on the sides. Billy got behind the wheel while Wiley got in the back, letting Kit sit up front.

Billy started the engine, switched on the wipers, and turned on the headlights. He could barely see out the windshield as the obscuring droplets covered the glass after each sweep of the blades.

Wiley sat forward in his seat. "Better take it nice and easy in this mess."

Even though the Medical Center was only a short distance away, it was anyone's guess how long it would take in the torrential downpour.

35

Penny couldn't stop shivering. She looked over at the thermostat gauge by the door and saw the needle was just above the forty degrees mark. Her arms weren't as cold as her bare legs as she was wearing a sweater. Sitting on the cooler, she wrapped her arms around the front of her legs to try and keep her body heat from escaping. Her butt felt like it was frozen to the plastic lid.

She checked her wristwatch and figured it had been almost an hour since the banging had stopped, and in that time, her boss hadn't spoken a word even though she had badgered him with questions.

Gordy stood against the far wall and hadn't moved since they had retreated inside. He was wearing a heavy down jacket with a fur-lined hood that he had grabbed before darting into the refrigeration unit. He didn't seem concerned that Penny was freezing to death in only her waitress uniform.

Cold vapors blew out their mouths and nostrils.

The walk-in freezer was a ten-by-ten-foot portable unit with thick insulation and ample shelving that could keep food frozen for a 24-hour period in the event the electricity should go out. Three large sides of beef hung from ceiling hooks.

"I can't stay in here any longer," Penny said and tried to get up off the cooler. The back of her thighs stuck to the lid. She gritted her teeth, put her hands on the edge of the lid, and pushed off. She winced as her skin stayed connected to the plastic for a brief second and then pulled free. She looked down expecting to see blood on the lid and was relieved to see she hadn't injured herself.

She walked over to the red emergency release pushpad on the door and hit it with the palm of her hand.

The heavy door should have popped open but it didn't.

Penny hit the pushpad again but still the door wouldn't open.

She turned to Gordy. "Don't just stand there, get us out of here."

Gordy reacted for the first time since they had trapped themselves inside the freezer. He came over, shoved her aside, and struck the emergency release pad.

Again, the door didn't budge.

"That thing must have damaged the release mechanism," Gordy said. He hit the door with his fist.

"That's not going to solve anything," Penny said, criticizing his actions.

"I suggest you shut up!"

"What's wrong with you Gordy? Why are you acting so strange?"

"Didn't I just tell you to keep your damn mouth shut?"

Penny backed away from her manic boss and went to sit back down on the cooler.

"And go over there," he said, pointing to the other side of the freezer where the beef ribs were hanging.

"Why can't I sit down here?"

"Just do it."

"What's inside these coolers?" Penny asked, staring down at the two blue ice chests.

"Never you mind."

Penny acted like she was going to comply with Gordy's order and began to turn then abruptly leaned down and lifted the lid on the cooler she had been sitting on.

She looked inside.

The plastic lining was smeared with blood and the meat stacked inside looked like it had been recently field dressed, as some of the slabs of meat still had strips of fur attached.

"My God. Is this what you've been serving our customers?" She spun around to confront Gordy but never had the chance as he swung a frozen box at her head.

36

Abel held the rear exit door open so that Grant and Dave could bring in the first corpse, which was Cindy Lambert. They entered the morgue, lifted her body bag off the gurney, and placed it on a table. The men went back outside to the van and returned with Bernie's body.

Dave looked around the room trying to figure where he could put Bernie as all four tables were currently being occupied by Ralph Tillerman, Bud Tinker, Danny Grimes, and of course, now Cindy.

Out of respect to his friend, Dave had put Ron Tully inside the only available roll-out drawer tucked in the wall, not adhering to the first-in-first-out rule of preserving corpses. "I guess they'll have to double up. Mind giving me a hand?"

"Sure," Grant said. They went over to the table with Bud Tinker's headless body, and together, lifted the carcass up and shifted it down so that there was four feet of room at the top. "What now?" he asked.

"We can put Ralph Tillerman there," Dave said.

Abel watched as they went over to a table with a body bag that bulged more in the middle. The ends were flat so the two men grabbed the loose plastic and lifted the body bag.

The contents sloshed inside.

Dave must have seen Abel's reaction to the sound because he said, "I had to scoop his insides off the floor and dump it in with the rest of him."

Grant and Dave swung the bag up on the end of the table next to Bud's sheet-covered body.

Abel went back into the hall and made sure the rear door was closed. He heard footsteps at the other end of the corridor.

Billy Boggs, Kit, and Wiley Tanner were walking towards him. They shook the rain from their clothes.

"What are you three doing out in this storm?" Abel asked.

"There's something running wild, terrorizing the town," Billy said. "Attacked some folks in the Food Mart."

"This thing sure gets around," Grant said, stepping out of the morgue doorway.

"Dad, it killed Macy Givens and Vern Thompson."

"Where's it now?"

"It ran off," Billy said. "Tim, Suzie Milcher, and Mr. Clemmens are dead too."

"I better get over there," Abel said.

"That's not all."

"No?"

"Damn Levitt brothers robbed my store," Wiley said. "Planned on burning down my place with me in it; that's until Billy showed up and put out the fire."

"Good for you, Billy," Abel said, praising the young man.

"Thanks, son," Grant said and smiled.

"Well, it never would have happened if I hadn't—"

"Gotten there a few minutes earlier," Wiley blurted, interrupting Billy and slapping him on the back before he could clear his conscience.

"Does this mean I should head over to the Food Mart?" Dave asked, standing in the doorway.

"Not just yet. I want to go upstairs and check with Kate."

"We might as all go. Kit and I haven't been to visit Bess," Grant said.

"All right," Abel said.

The five of them headed up the stairwell while Dave remained downstairs and readied the gurney for more bodies.

As soon as they opened the fire door onto the second floor, Grant, Wiley, and Kit headed over to Bess' room. Billy hung back and walked over to the nursing station with the sheriff.

"Where's Kate?" Abel asked Vera.

"In her office."

"I'll be right back," Abel told Billy.

Abel went down the hall and stuck his head through the open doorway. Kate was at her desk, reviewing a patient's folder. She looked up when she heard him knock on the doorjamb.

"Can you go with Dave to the supermarket?" he asked.

"Why?"

"There's been some trouble. Some people were killed and there might be some that need medical attention."

"Have you called Bill?"

"Not yet. Do you think you could?"

"Sure," Kate said. "Aren't you going?"

"I'll be there when I can. But first, I have to find and arrest Halsey and Rand Levitt."

"Why, what did they do?"

"Broke into the hardware store and almost killed Wiley."

"My God. Okay, I'll call Bill right away and ride over there with him."

"Good. Where's Cooper?"

"Right over there," Kate said and pointed to the German shepherd sitting in the corner of the office.

"Hey, boy," Abel said then turned to Kate. "Make sure he stays in here."

"I will."

Abel stepped into the office. He came around the desk, bent down, and kissed Kate.

"Wow, what got into you?" she responded after their lips parted.

Abel gave her a smile. "Just making my rounds. I best go."

"You be careful."

Billy was still standing by the nursing station when Abel returned.

"Why aren't you in visiting with everyone?" he asked the young man.

"Mrs. Tanner doesn't like me much."

"Oh? That all might change once she hears what you did to save the store."

"I don't think so."

Abel turned when he heard footsteps. Grant and Kit were leaving Bess' room and coming over to the nursing station.

"You going after the Levitts?" Grant asked.

"That's right," Abel replied.

"I'm going with you."

"All right."

"Ah jeez," Billy said. "I nearly forgot."

"Forgot what?" Abel asked.

"I was supposed to go back to work, help Penny close up. Only I don't have a ride."

"Take my Grandpa's car," Kit said. "I'm sure he'll trust you with it. He plans on staying here awhile with my mom anyway."

"Are you sure it's okay?"

"Sure. I'll come with you."

"You two be safe out there," Abel said.

"We will," Billy said as he and Kit headed down the hall.

"We better get going," Abel said to Grant.

"This sure has been one strange night."

"You're telling me."

37

"Where are we going?" Rand said, glancing out the rear window of the truck to see if any cars were following them. "We already got our stuff from the house."

"Gordy still owes us money," Halsey replied. After leaving the Tanner store, they had gone home and hurriedly packed up some of their belongings. He figured Wiley was dead by now and the place was gutted from the fire and hopefully still burning despite the heavy rain. It had been the ideal distraction for a perfect getaway.

They'd collected Cobb and Grover and put them in the back of the truck with plans to bury them up at the cabin.

Halsey pulled the truck into the parking lot behind the Porterville Steakhouse and parked next to Gordy's pickup.

"What if he doesn't want to pay up?" Rand asked.

"Then we kill him and help ourselves."

"You think that's a good idea? I mean robbing old man Tanner and setting fire to his place and making it look like an accident was one thing but killing Gordy? I don't know."

"Hey, you were ready to gun down the game warden."

"Yeah, well, that was different."

"How so?"

"He was messing with our livelihood."

"Well, you better hope then that Gordy pays us."

Halsey turned off the engine and climbed out of the driver's side. He had to hold onto the door or get blown off his feet. He pushed the door closed and held onto the top railing of the bed as he made his way around to the rear bumper.

Rand had gotten out and was leaning into the rain as he headed for the back of the building. He pulled open the rear door and held on so that it didn't swing back in the wind and crash against the exterior wall. Halsey entered the restaurant with Rand right behind, struggling but still able to close the door, the noise masked by the sound of the violent storm outside.

It was almost pitch dark.

"Must have lost their power," Halsey said. He reached inside his pocket and took out a cigarette lighter. He flipped it open and flicked the wheel. A small blue flame lit up. It was enough light that he could see about ten feet either way.

"Think everyone's gone home?" Rand asked.

"Don't know," Halsey replied then yelled out, "Hey, Gordy! You in here?"

A second later, they heard pounding.

"Where's that coming from?" Rand said.

"Sounds like the walk-in freezer." Halsey walked over to the dented metal door. "Will you look at that? Looks like someone took a sledgehammer to it."

The pounding continued on the opposite side of the door.

"Is that you Gordy?"

They could hear a muffled reply.

"What'd he do? Get locked inside?" Rand said and laughed.

"Dumb ass thing to do." Halsey reached down and grabbed the door handle half-expecting it to be locked but was surprised when the latch disengaged and the door swung open.

Gordy stepped out. Even though he was wearing a heavy jacket, he was still rubbing his arms and shoulders to get warm.

Halsey glanced inside the walk-in freezer and saw the waitress lying on the floor. "She dead?"

"Pretty damn close," Gordy said.

"Do we leave her in there?" Rand asked his brother.

"I would," Gordy said. "Unless you want her blabbing about our little operation."

"She knows?" Halsey asked.

"Not exactly, but she suspects something was up when she looked inside one of those coolers."

"What were you doing in there?" Rand asked.

"That thing attacked the restaurant so we ducked in here. Then it started beating on the door. Must have screwed up the lock 'cause we couldn't open the door from the inside."

Halsey pushed the door closed and turned to Gordy. "Do you have a flashlight? This lighter is burning the hell out of my hand."

"Yeah, I have one right here." Gordy flicked on the flashlight in his hand and shined it on the floor.

"Good," Halsey said. "Now give us our money."

"I made a run to the bank yesterday so there's no money here except for what's out in the register."

"Don't lie to me," Halsey said and pulled a handgun out from under his coat.

Rand reached in his pocket and drew a revolver. "You better listen to my brother."

"I know you have a safe in your office. We're not here to rob you blind. We just want what's coming to us."

"All right. But not a penny more."

"Don't rile me Gordy or we'll take it all and use you for target practice."

Gordy didn't say any more. He shined the light down the walkthrough as they passed the kitchen and went into his office. He went over to a picture hanging on the wall of a massive heifer bull and removed it, exposing a combination safe tucked inside the wood paneling. He turned the dial back and forth a few times until the locked clicked then opened the safe door. He began to reach inside.

"Not so fast, Gordy. Step away," Halsey ordered.

The restaurant owner did what he was told and moved back.

Halsey walked over. He put his hand inside the safe and took out a small semi-automatic pistol. "Nice try. Never figured you'd have a lady's gun."

"Hey, I wasn't going to use it. Hell, I forgot it was even there."

"Sure, Gordy." Halsey reached in with both hands and pulled out large stacks of money wrapped in rubber bands. He placed them on Gordy's desk. He grabbed a single stack and flipped through the bills to get an idea of how much each was worth.

"This should do it," Halsey said and picked up half of what was there.

"Hey!" Gordy protested.

"Or would you rather we took it all?"

"Fine. Take it."

"You know, you might think about leaving town. We are."

"Looks like I'm not going to have much of a choice, seeing as I killed my waitress and my restaurant was destroyed by that thing of yours."

"Well, I wouldn't exactly call it mine," Halsey said.

"Shit, Halsey," Rand said. "We better get out of here before it comes back."

"You're right. Well, Gordy, it's been nice doing business with you." Halsey grinned and held up the fat stack of money.

"Wish I could say the same."

Halsey and Rand raced through the kitchen and bolted out the back door into the rain.

38

Billy and Kit were just pulling into the front parking lot of the steakhouse when Billy had to swerve out of the way or Halsey would have plowed into them with his big truck.

They heard a siren, looked out the rear window, and saw Sheriff McGuire racing down the main road with the emergency lights flashing. Halsey skidded the truck onto the wet pavement and headed up the mountain road with the sheriff in hot pursuit.

"They're in trouble now," Kit said as Billy parked in front of the restaurant.

The rain was coming down pretty heavy so they got out quickly and ran for cover below the overhang. Billy glanced down the walkway and saw a pair of women's shoes pointed toe-first on the cement, protruding beyond a parked car just outside a broken-out restaurant window. "There's someone lying over here." He approached slowly, Kit by his side.

"Oh my God, that's Donna Rice!" Kit yelled. Even though the woman was flat on her stomach with her arms at her side, palms up, they could see her face as her head had been twisted halfway around, her open eyes staring blankly up at the night sky.

"We better get inside," Billy said. When they went to the front entrance, they saw the door had been smashed open.

"Billy, you don't think that thing's in here?"

"I hope not. Stay close." They stepped inside the restaurant.

"Oh my God, are they all dead?"

"Looks that way," Billy said, spotting the two sets of legs sticking out from under the crumbled table weighted down by the heavy wall mirror. He looked down at the body under the newspaper machine. "If that's Donna Rice outside, that must be her husband."

Kit gasped when she saw Hardin Lee hanging on the deer antlers.

They heard an engine start up and looked out the window. Gordy's Ford truck raced by the parked cars, turned onto the main road, and disappeared into the night.

"He's sure in big a hurry to get out of here," Billy said and gave Kit a wary look.

"Where's Penny? Think she left already?"

"I don't think so. Her car's still out front. We better check in the back."

They walked across the trashed dining area, careful not to step in any of the pools of blood saturating the carpet.

"Look, there's Penny's purse," Billy said, spotting her bag under the counter.

Billy led the way into the kitchen. They walked past the large griddle.

"What happened there?" Kit said once she saw the dented-up door on the walk-in freezer.

"Looks like something was trying to get in." Billy grabbed the handle and opened the door. "Oh my God, Penny!" he yelled when he saw his co-worker lying on the cold floor.

"Is she dead?"

Billy knelt beside Penny and felt her neck. "No, I can feel a pulse but it's weak. Help me carry her out."

Kit came in and grabbed Penny's feet while Billy hoisted her up by her arms.

They brought her out to the dining room and lowered her down on a clean patch of carpet. Kit immediately took off her coat and placed it over the unconscious woman while Billy gathered up some tablecloths to use as blankets. They each took one of Penny's hands and vigorously rubbed them to get the circulation flowing.

Billy reached up and grabbed a couple of candleholders off the tables, placed them on the floor, and lit them so they could have some light. "Should we give her CPR or something?"

"I don't know, is she breathing?"

Billy leaned his ear down over Penny's nose and mouth. "Yeah, she is."

"Then I think we have to keep her warm and get her to the hospital."

"I'll pull the car up to the entrance and we can carry her out."

Billy was about to get to his feet when he saw Penny slowly opening her eyes.

"Penny, don't worry, you're going to be okay," Billy said, doing his best to hold back the tears.

She looked up and gave him a weak smile. "Billy, you came back."

39

Abel managed to stay in control of the Crown Victoria despite the pouring down rain and having to slosh over the muddy roads as they chased after the Levitt's monster truck. At times, they were going so fast the front bumper of the police cruiser had almost gone under the rear bumper of the high-suspension truck.

The brothers clearly had the advantage as their vehicle had four-wheel drive and all-terrain tires, not to mention they had a destination in mind and knew the logging roads like a salmon knows the route to its spawning pool.

So it wasn't surprising when Abel finely lost them.

He kept the high beams on as the cruiser headed up yet another logging road. He drove with one hand on the steering wheel, the other directing the spotlight on the trees to his left as they searched for Halsey's truck.

He panned the light on a thick clump of bushes that didn't seem natural. "Grant, does that look right to you?"

As soon as the car stopped, Grant jumped out. He went around the front of the car and rushed over to the high mound of shrubs. He grabbed some branches and yanked out an entire bush. He tossed it aside and removed another uprooted shrub that had been stacked as camouflage to conceal the side road. As soon as he had cleared a path wide enough for the car, he hurried back to the cruiser and jumped in.

Abel gunned the Crown Victoria up the narrow track that edged up through the trees. They hadn't gone more than a hundred yards when they saw a small rustic cabin and a yellowish glow in a window.

"I never knew the Levitts had a cabin up here," Grant said, pointing to Halsey's monster truck parked in a turnaround.

"There's probably a lot we don't know." Abel switched off the headlights and his spotlight. He coasted up beside the truck and parked so that the cruiser wouldn't be seen if someone were to look out from the cabin window. The last thing he wanted was for someone inside the cabin to ambush them as they were getting out of the car.

They got out slowly, closed the doors quietly, and drew their side arms.

Abel and Grant moved around to the big truck's rear bumper. Abel snuck a peek at the cabin. There was no one at the window. He checked the surrounding trees by the cabin but didn't see anyone lurking in the shadows.

But that didn't mean they weren't there.

"What do you think?" Abel asked.

"Knowing Halsey, the place could be booby trapped."

"Then we better watch where we step."

They crept toward the cabin.

Abel caught sight of something at the base of a tree about twenty feet from the front porch. He signaled to Grant and they went over to see what it was.

Even with his face bashed in, they knew it was Cobb Levitt lying there in the mud. The bulldog was next to him. It was almost as if they'd laid down on the ground for a nap. Two shovels were propped up against the tree trunk.

They headed over to the cabin and went up the three steps to the porch. Instead of knocking, Abel tried the doorknob. It was unlocked.

He turned the handle and nudged the door open. The first thing he noticed was the god-awful smell that was so strong that it made his eyes water.

A single kerosene lamp provided the only lighting inside the one-room cabin and was situated on a long table positioned on the other side of the room. Halsey was standing at the table with his back turned. A rifle was leaning against a chair within easy reach.

Abel stepped in first. "Halsey, it's Sheriff McGuire. I suggest when you turn around, you do it nice and slow, and don't reach for your gun. You're under arrest for burglary, arson, and attempted murder."

Halsey raised his hands level with his shoulders.

Grant came in and stood next to Abel. "God almighty, what's that smell?"

"I don't know but it's making my eyes burn." Abel took another step and kept his gun pointed at Halsey who hadn't turned around and remained frozen in the same position.

Abel could hear something whimpering down behind the table.

"What do you have back there?" Abel said.

"Maybe you should come over and have a look," Halsey replied. He turned around slowly and had a big grin on his face.

Before Abel could ask him what he thought was so amusing, a voice behind them said, "Drop the guns or the game warden gets it first." Rand Levitt stepped out from behind the door and aimed his hunting rifle at Grant's head.

"I'd do as he says. Rand's not too keen on men in uniform," Halsey said.

Abel and Grant dropped their weapons on the floor.

"Now move over there," Rand said and prodded Grant in the back with the muzzle of his gun.

Abel got a better look at what was on the tabletop as they walked to the middle of the room. "What do you have there? Bearskins?"

"You know bear hunting is against the law," Grant said.

"Is that right."

From where he stood, Abel could see the corner of a large cage just under the table. Something was moving around inside. "So what do you have there, a bear cub?"

"Oh, it's something much better than that."

Grant stepped over to the table. "There has to be over ten hides here." He grabbed the top pelt, dragged it off the heap, and laid the animal skin out flat on the floor. "Jesus, this thing had to have been eight feet tall."

"That'd be about right," Halsey gloated.

"Guess we can go ahead and show them," Rand said, keeping his rifle trained on Abel and Grant. "Seeing as they're going to be dead soon anyhow."

"Step around and enjoy the show," Halsey said. He moved to the other side of the table.

When it saw Abel, the small, furry creature stood up in the cage and grabbed the bars with both hands.

"Jesus, Halsey. That can't be what I think it is."

"Oh, it is."

"You've captured a baby Bigfoot?"

"That's right."

Grant glared at Halsey and pointed at the pelts on the table. "And these?"

"As you can see, we've been hunting them for some time."

"Killing Bigfoot! Do you know how much trouble you're in?" Grant said.

"It's not like they're an endangered species or anything. Damn things aren't even supposed to exist."

"And what are you planning on doing with this one?" Abel asked, looking down at the cage.

"Figuring on selling it on the Internet to the highest bidder. I'm sure there're plenty of people out there willing to pay big money for this cuddly Sasquatch."

The baby Bigfoot glared at Halsey and growled.

"Yeah, I guess I'd be mad too, if someone wiped out my family."

"So you're the reason it's been terrorizing the town," Abel said. "It's looking for this youngster."

"Damn thing's got one hell of a nose, I'll give it that."

"Yeah, following your blood trail," Abel said.

Halsey shrugged. He grabbed a cloth sack off the table and tossed it to Grant.

"What's this?" Grant asked. He opened the bag and looked inside. "Jesus, Halsey. What is this, jerky?"

"Sure is. Try it. Smoked it myself."

"You stupid son of a bitch," Grant said and lunged at Halsey. Rand aimed his rifle at the game warden and shot him in the back. Grant stumbled forward and fell to the floor.

Abel turned just as the front door smashed open, swinging so hard against the wall that it broke off the hinges.

The beast punched out the boards around the doorframe so it could fit its enormous body through the doorway.

Rand spun around with his rifle.

The beast grabbed the barrel and ripped the weapon from his hands.

Rand's eyes bulged as he stared up at the monstrous creature and crossed his arms in front of his face.

The beast grabbed Rand's right arm. With a forceful tug, it wrenched the limb clear out of the socket and threw the appendage against the wall.

Rand screamed as blood spurted from the hole in his shoulder like water gushing out of a ruptured fire hydrant.

Halsey scrambled around the table for his rifle.

Abel moved back, the beast now between him and his gun. He looked down at Grant laying facedown on the floor and saw his friend's right hand move.

Halsey snatched up his rifle, but before he could get a bead on the massive creature, the beast grabbed Rand by his other arm and hurled him across the room.

The rifle discharged and shattered the kerosene lamp just as Rand crashed into his brother. Both men were knocked unconscious and crumbled to the floor.

Liquid fire spilled out onto the table, igniting the pelts.

The beast took a plank-splitting step then stopped when it saw the fire starting to spread. There were scars on its face and body, places were big chunks of fur and flesh had been ripped off, leaving blackened wounds that had healed over badly. Abel wondered if this was the creature Bess Tanner had struck with her car. It looked like it had been through hell and back, and probably had.

Raging flames swept down off the table and engulfed the Levitt brothers still knocked cold on the floorboards.

Abel glanced over at the cage and saw a pitiful little face staring back. He went over and unlatched the door to the wire enclosure.

The youngster cowered, too afraid to move as the cabin filled up with smoke.

"It's okay, you can go," Abel said with a degree of assurance, knowing time was running out and the cabin would soon become an inferno.

The beast grunted and made a few gruff noises, which seemed to get the youngster's attention.

"Time to scat, little fella," Abel said. He bent down and gently coaxed the animal out of the cage. "Go, shoo."

The thick and blinding smoke was making it difficult to breathe.

Abel could hear the tiny feet scurrying across the hot floor.

The beast scooped up its terrified offspring with one hand and held it protectively against its massive chest. It looked at Abel and let out a deep huff before lumbering out of the burning cabin.

By then, Abel's hair and clothes were smoldering. He rolled Grant over onto his back and grabbed him under the armpits. He dragged him across the floor through the raging fire, stopping for a second to collect their handguns then continuing out the front door.

The rain quickly extinguished the embers clinging to their clothes.

Abel was surprised to see Grant still clutching onto the sack of jerky and suddenly thought of the ramifications having it in their possession. He glanced around in a panic then let out a sigh of relief.

The beast and its youngster were long gone.

40

"Isn't this something? I finally get discharged and you're in here occupying the very bed I was in," Bess Tanner said, standing next to Grant's hospital bed.

"Thanks for keeping it warm for me," Grant said and winced when he tried to smile.

Kate was standing at the foot of the bed, examining Grant's chart. "You're lucky that bullet went clear through just under your shoulder and didn't hit anything vital."

Abel was leaning against the wall by the door. "We were both lucky to get out of there alive."

"What about Halsey and Rand?" Grant asked.

"Didn't make it."

"Can't say as I'm too broken up. How long have I been out?"

"About thirty-six hours," Kate said. She glanced over at Abel. "I'm going to check on my other patients and then I'll be ready to go."

"Sure thing," Abel said as Kate stepped out of the room.

"I'll leave you two alone," Bess said. "Wiley and Kit are waiting for me out in the hall." She bent down and kissed Grant on the forehead. "Hurry up and get well."

"I'll do my best," he replied.

"Thanks for everything," Bess said to Abel and gave him a kiss on the cheek before leaving the room.

"So, what did I miss?" Grant asked. He picked up the control pad lying on the blanket, pushed a button, and raised his bed a bit so he was sitting up.

"Well, from what I can gather, the Levitt brothers were killing Bigfoot and selling the meat to Gordy Oxman."

"You mean he was serving that to his customers?"

"That's right. I had Lucy Banks run a comparison test using the jerky Halsey had in that bag and the meat samples we found in some coolers in the freezer at the steakhouse. They turned out to be a positive match."

"Where is Gordy?"

"Not sure. I put an APB out on him for attempted murder as he assaulted Penny and left her in the freezer. I imagine the state troopers will be catching up to him soon."

"So how many people did it kill?"

"As far as I can tell, almost twenty. I have a hunch that the victims were anyone that had eaten or just handled the meat. Billy and Peggy never ate there but they'd both been in direct contact with the meat, serving and cleaning up. Would explain why it spared Kit at the supermarket."

"Who would guess eating your veggies could make the difference between life and death?" Grant said. "So what now?"

"Well, I'm still working on the police report and haven't shared much of the case with anyone. You know if it weren't for the Levitt brothers going up there and slaughtering those Bigfoot, none of this would ever have happened."

"And if folks think there's more of them up there on the mountain, they're going to want to go up there and kill every one of them just so they can have their revenge."

"Which is the last thing I want," Abel said. "There's been enough killing. No, I have a better idea."

"What's that?"

"I'll file my report and say the beast died in the fire along with the Levitt brothers, case closed."

"You'd lie," Grant said.

"If it meant saving lives—yes."

"All right, then that's how it happened." Grant yawned. "Well, if you don't mind, I think I'm going catch twenty winks before Vera comes in with my lunch tray."

"You take care, Grant," Abel said, starting for the door.

"Abel?"

The sheriff stopped and turned around.

"Thanks," Grant said.

"Anytime," Abel replied and walked out of the room.

As he approached the nursing station, he saw Bess smiling with her good arm around Billy's shoulder. Wiley and Kit were smiling too.

"Enjoy your afternoon," Abel said.

"We will," Kit answered for everyone. "Grandpa is going to give Billy a full-time job at his store."

"Congratulations, Billy."

"Thanks, Sheriff."

"He deserves it, after what he did saving Wiley and Kit," Bess said. She looked at Billy. "I was wrong to misjudge you. Do you forgive me?"

Billy nodded and gave her a big smile.

"Who knows, might have a mind to make the boy store manager," Wiley said.

"That's even better." Abel gave them a wave and walked down the hall to Kate's office. Cooper was lying on the floor with his chin on his front paws, tail wagging as he'd heard Abel approaching.

"Come on, Coop, time to go."

The Alsatian jumped to his feet and rushed to the door.

Abel bent down to pet the dog but the canine kept going. Turning, he saw Kate a few feet away and Cooper licking her hand.

"You know, I might stop bringing him around if he's going to get all the attention."

"Well, Sheriff. How about when we get home I give you some?" Kate said.

"Sounds good to me."

41

One year later...

The 36-foot fishing trawler skimmed silently across the calm waters of the Monterey Bay, having been out for most of the night. The boat was virtually invisible, as it crept ominously through the fog bank like a ghostly apparition toward the shrouded shoreline and harbor.

The skipper was at the helm, his two crewmembers standing watch outside. The seamen wore black, woolen watch caps, foul weather jackets, and knee-high rubber boots.

As the running lights were intentionally turned off, the skipper and his crew had to be especially vigilant to avoid a maritime collision, though it was doubtful that any other boats would be out on the water in such dense fog.

Using an exposed spire of a tall smoke stack from the power plant as a landmark, the skipper steered down a narrow waterway into a dredged canal.

Up ahead was the ramshackle cannery.

The mast of the boat just cleared the underside of the pitched metal roof as the vessel entered the inlet inside the abandoned warehouse.

The skipper powered down the boat as the crew secured the mooring lines to the dock.

Pigeons fluttered their wings in the high rafters of the large building once used by commercial fisheries for cleaning and packaging ocean fish, which in those days were brought in by the boatloads.

Now the structure was a place for birds to roost and surreptitious enterprises.

A sailor started up the winch on the boom lift control box.

The boom stretching out over the stern began to rise and the outriggers collected up the fishnets into one humongous, dripping ball as it was hoisted out of the water and swung out over the port side onto the dock.

The skipper and his men stepped down off the boat, walked over, and stared in amazement at the dead sea creature tangled up in the nets.

Finally, the skipper said, "All right men. Enough of the lollygagging—we've got work to do."

42

Sam Winters, his wife, Kelly, and their six-year-old son, Gabe, were having the time of their lives, enjoying their mini-vacation on the coast. The day before they had gone out on a whale-watching cruise. As his son had never been out in a boat before, Sam made sure Gabe took a Dramamine a couple of hours before the tour began. As an added precaution, Kelly brought along a box of saltine crackers to settle their stomachs in the event anyone felt seasick.

It had been a beautiful, clear day with plenty of sky and hardly any clouds, which made the ocean's surface especially blue. Perfect for spotting blowhole gushes and flukes splashing down.

There had been in the upwards of twenty people on board and everyone seemed to want to congregate up front, as the bow of the boat offered the best view.

A few times, the sightseeing boat had rocked back and forth as it hit choppy water from a wake left by another nearby passing craft. As the deck dipped, everyone, including Sam, Kelly, and Gabe would stagger over to the lower side of the boat and up against the handrail, which wasn't any higher than three feet tall and was especially scary as someone could easily be pitched over the side. It was a miracle no one had fallen overboard.

Today, they had just finished visiting the Monterey Bay Aquarium. Gabe had been especially excited having just watched *Finding Dory* as many of the scenes depicted in the animated movie were based on the actual place. There had been so much to see and do.

Gabe had fun playing in the intertidal exhibit, touching the different starfishes. Sam loved watching his son marvel at the giant tank of jellyfish and got a kick out of seeing the look on his boy's face when they came to the 28-foot-tall pane of glass with the kelp forest undulating in the current on the opposite side.

Sam's favorite had been seeing a great white shark close enough that he might have felt its sandpapery skin if it wasn't for the seven-inch-thick glass separating the two.

Kelly couldn't get enough of the sea otter exhibit as she often said that if she had to come back as an animal, it would be as this adorable marine animal.

It was late in the afternoon and everyone was hungry. Sam had read about a new seafood restaurant that had recently opened on the pier and suggested they should give it a try.

There was a short line outside that ran along the side of the small restaurant. An employee was standing at a podium by the door up front, writing down names.

While Kelly went up to reserve a table, Sam and Gabe waited in line. There was a glass display case on the exterior wall with black and white photographs of what the cannery looked like during the years when it was operational. A three-page historical background and a list of interesting facts pertaining to Monterey Bay were thumbtacked to a sheet of corkboard.

Sam picked up Gabe so the boy could get a closer look at the pictures.

Kelly came back and got in line. "Anything interesting?"

"I'll say. Says here there are places in the Monterey Bay with depths up to two miles and that the subterranean canyon is so big, you could fit two Grand Canyons inside of it."

"Well, I'm glad we've crossed whale-watching off of our list of things to do."

"Hey, Dad! What's that ugly thing?" Gabe said, pointing at an old photograph of a prehistoric-looking sea creature that had washed ashore onto the beach. There was only a shot of its head and a portion of its long neck. The mouth was long, duck-billed but fleshier and rounded instead of flat. The men standing in the background seemed diminutive in comparison.

Sam scanned the short article beneath the snapshot. "This picture was taken in 1925. Some scientists believed the creature might have been a plesiosaurus. It was called the Monster of Monterey Bay. Later, people developed a fondest for it and named it Bobo, and was thought to be much like the legendary Loch Ness Monster, Nessie."

There was also an artist's illustration comparing the size of a man in increments of feet with the prehistoric animal. The plesiosaurus measured fifty feet from the tip of its nose to the end of its tail, the length of its neck a good twenty feet long. It had a fat lizard-like body with a ten-foot-long tail and flippers instead of legs.

The line started moving quickly and it wasn't long before they were seated at a table by a window with a grand view of the bay. They could see sea lions lazing on the rocks and fishing boats out on the water.

The waitress brought them glasses of water and menus.

After perusing the entrees, Sam glanced over at Gabe. "Can you believe there's even a Bobo burger on the menu?"

"Really, Dad. I want one."

"It does look good," Kelly said. "I think I'll have that, too."

When the waitress came over to take their orders, Sam told her it was unanimous and they were having the Bobo burgers and fries.

Sam and Gabe gazed out the window and watched a man wearing a black wetsuit drifting by on a paddleboard, propelling himself with a long-handled oar.

Before they knew it, their waitress was back with three red baskets, each with a thick Bobo burger and crispy french fries.

Sam picked up his bun and took a bite. "Hmm, this is really good."

He waited as Kelly and Gabe dove into their burgers. They both looked at Sam and smiled with their mouths full. Gabe even had a little grease running down his chin.

Sam took a moment and wiped his mouth with a napkin. He saw a man coming from the restrooms, walking between the tables. He was wearing a short order cook's paper hat, a white T-shirt, and a long apron that went down past his knees.

As the man neared their table, Sam glanced up and said, "I have to say these Bobo burgers are excellent. Please give our regards to the cook."

"I'll be sure to pass that along," Gordy Oxman said with a big grin and continued back to the kitchen.

THE END

ABOUT THE AUTHOR

Gerry Griffiths lives in San Jose, California, with his family and their five rescue dogs and a cat. He is a Horror Writers Association member, has over thirty published short stories in various anthologies and magazines, as well as a short story collection entitled *Creatures*. He is also the author of *Silurid* and *The Beasts of Stoneclad Mountain*, as well as *Death Crawlers* with the follow-up standalone novels, *Deep in the Jungle* and *The Next World*, all published by Severed Press.

CHECK OUT OTHER GREAT HORROR NOVELS

CHECK OUT OTHER GREAT HORROR NOVELS

DEATH CRAWLERS
by Gerry Griffiths

Worldwide, there are thought to be 8,000 species of centipede, of which, only 3,000 have been scientifically recorded. The venom of Scolopendra gigantea—the largest of the arthropod genus found in the Amazon rainforest—is so potent that it is fatal to small animals and toxic to humans. But when a cargo plane departs the Amazon region and crashes inside a national park in the United States, much larger and deadlier creatures escape the wreckage to roam wild, reproducing at an astounding rate. Entomologist, Frank Travis solicits small town sheriff Wanda Rafferty's help and together they investigate the crash site. But as a rash of gruesome deaths befalls the townsfolk of Prospect, Frank and Wanda will soon discover how vicious and cunning these new breed of predators can be. Meanwhile, Jake and Nora Carver, and another backpacking couple, are venturing up into the mountainous terrain of the park. If only they knew their fun-filled weekend is about to become a living nightmare.

THE PULLER
by Michael Hodges

Matt Kearns has two choices: fight or hide. The creature in the orchard took the rest. Three days ago, he arrived at his favorite place in the world, a remote shack in Michigan's Upper Peninsula. The plan was to mourn his father's death and figure out his life. Now he's fighting for it. An invisible creature has him trapped. Every time Matt tries to flee, he's dragged backwards by an unseen force. Alone and with no hope of rescue, Matt must escape the Puller's reach. But how do you free yourself from something you cannot see?

CHECK OUT OTHER GREAT
HORROR NOVELS

BLACK FRIDAY
by Michael Hodges

Jared the kleptomaniac, Chike the unemployed IT guy, Patricia the shopaholic, and Jeff the meth dealer are trapped inside a Chicago supermall on Black Friday. Bridgefield Mall empties during a fire alarm, and most of the shoppers drive off into a strange mist surrounding the mall parking lot. They never return. Chike and his group try calling friends and family, but their smart phones won't work, not even Twitter. As the mist creeps closer, the mall lights flicker and surge. Bulbs shatter and spray glass into the air. Unsettling noises are heard from within the mist, as the meth dealer becomes unhinged and hunts the group within the mall. Cornered by the mist, and hunted from within, Chike and the survivors must fight for their lives while solving the mystery of what happened to Bridgefield Mall. Sometimes, a good sale just isn't worth it.

GRIMWEAVE
by Tim Curran

In the deepest, darkest jungles of Indochina, an ancient evil is waiting in a forgotten, primeval valley. It is patient, monstrous, and bloodthirsty. Perfectly adapted to its hot, steaming environment, it strikes silent and stealthy, it chosen prey: human. Now Michael Spiers, a Marine sniper, the only survivor of a previous encounter with the beast, is going after it again. Against his better judgement, he is made part of a Marine Force Recon team that will hunt it down and destroy it.

The hunters are about to become the hunted.

www.ingramcontent.com/pod-product-compliance
Lightning Source LLC
Chambersburg PA
CBHW051958170626
46808CB00007B/2684